BOBBY
AND
SARGE
ON THE HOMEFRONT

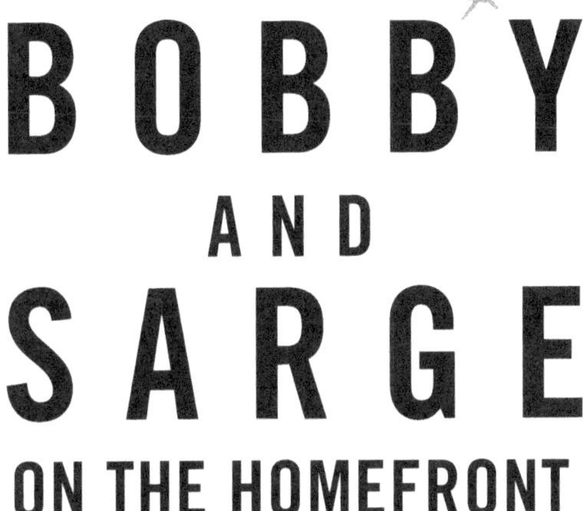

BOBBY
AND
SARGE
ON THE HOMEFRONT

MARY L. ROUTH-BRODIE

author of *Laura Ann and the Nazi Spy*

Bobby and Sarge

For information about this title or to order other books
and/or electronic media, contact the publisher:

Mary L. Routh-Brodie
mlbrodie776@gmail.com

ISBNs:
978-1-7355530-2-3 (print)
978-1-7355530-3-0 (eBook)

Printed in the United States of America

Cover and Interior design: 1106 Design

Dedicated to my sister, Sharon Routh Walker,
Who was my first audience, inspiration and continuing fan.
Thanks for always being there; my favorite Baby Boomer.
I love you.

ACKNOWLEDGMENTS

Thanks to my brother, Jack Routh, who constructed many WWII plane models and hung them from his bedroom ceiling. I still visualize them, and your worktable covered with papers, pins and glue. I should have told you then how neat they were.

My deepest appreciation to fellow World War II authors, who are so dedicated and precise in their own research. Shot Down by Steve Snyder, and A Higher Call by Adam Makos were especially helpful. A Woman of No Importance by Sonia Purnell offered information about the French Resistance, which led my investigation into the Shelbourne Line escape Route. Online state and federal archive sites provided accurate facts and photos of the WWII military hospital in Brigham City, Utah, a forerunner in several areas such as emotional and physical therapy and rehabilitation.

My own disclaimer is that I invented the use of vans and buses to provide families with transportation to visit the hospital. I had to get them there somehow as travel was so restricted.

Much admiration is due to those Americans who fought and died during WWII, and to those who came home wounded and damaged; also to the citizens, both old and young, who did what needed to be done on the Home Front.

My appreciation goes once again to 1106 Design for their efforts on my part to see this novel published.

To the young people and adults who joined Laura Ann, on her adventure in "Laura Ann and the Nazi Spy" and are willing to accompany "Bobby and Sarge" in the new novel. Perhaps you will realize more vividly how it was on the home front during WWII.

CONTENTS

GLOSSARY

Pan Am: Pan-American World Airlines was an important airlines in the first half of the 1900s

Focke-Wolf: A German warplane of WWII

The SS: Schutzstaffel; Dreaded organization of Nazi Germany, begun as Hitler's bodyguard unit. Wore black uniforms with skull and lightning-bolt insignias.

Luftwaffe: German air force

Dulag Luft: Prisoner of War camp for captured airmen.

Krauts: American slang name for Germans

OSS: Office of Strategic Services, precursor to the CIA.

Shelbourne Line: Escape route set up to guide downed Allied personnel to safety and transport to England.

MIA: Missing in Action

Service flag: Banners hung in American windows for those fighting overseas. Stars were stitched on them to show someone in that family had a person serving (blue), silver (MIA), or gold (killed).

GERMAN WORDS AND PHRASES:

Vas ist los?: What's happening?

Danke Schoen: Thank you.

Alles gut: Everything is okay.

Nicht kennt: I don't know.

Liebchen: term of endearment, like "sweetheart."

Meine Freundin: my friend (girl)

Kinder: children.

Wienerschnitzel: hot dog, sausage

Kuchen: cake

Ich auch: Me, too.

CHAPTER 1

Somewhere over France

January 1944

Somewhere over the coast of France, Captain Buzz Bradley glanced at the fuel gauge of his P-47 Thunderbolt. "Okay, Billie Jo." He patted the instrument panel. "Our testing's all done. Fly us back over the Channel." He drummed the side window with a knuckle for good luck and gave a quick salute to his wingman, Smitty.

The two men had become flying partners and fast friends during their piloting days for Pan Am in Brownsville, Texas. They went on to develop instrument techniques for that airline. After the war gobbled them up, Buzz and Smitty continued teaching those techniques at airfields in Britain and testing them in the unsettled skies over England and the Channel. Thus far, encounters with the German *Luftwaffe* had been limited.

1

"At two and ten," squawked his headpiece. Buzz scanned the heavy clouds. German planes emerged from the cloud cover, guns set on them. "Where did those rascals come from?" Buzz muttered as he readied to take on the one at two o'clock.

Smitty homed in on the one at ten. Maneuvering up, down, left, and right, Smitty got the drop on his adversary and watched as the German plane went down in flames. "Sorry, buddy," he said softly, "Better you than me."

Buzz was having his own *dogfight* with the other plane. Bullets pierced his right window as he banked to fly under the enemy plane, releasing a blast of machine gun fire. Ignoring minor damage to his own P-47, Buzz pursued the other. Twisting and turning, the Focke-Wulf disappeared into a thick layer of cloud. "Smart move, fella. I'm not chasing you into that."

Banking to catch up with Smitty and continue home, Buzz knuckled the window again. "You're not hurt much, Billie Jo," he said. "Let's go home."

At that instant, machine-gun fire raked the left side of the cockpit from above. "Sneaky bugger," Buzz growled. All senses fully alert, he maneuvered his own plane into the dance of *twist and turn*.

Years of training kicked in. Fly low. *Come on, follow me down. With any luck, you won't be able to pull out of your dive.*

"Eat dirt, Hansi!" Buzz yelled as he skimmed the treetops. But the German had no taste for dirt and swooped away.

Buzz glanced at his fuel gauge. His heart skipped a beat as he swore under his breath. "Bullets must've hit the fuel line. I'll have to ditch over land." He scanned the waves for the coastline of France and flew inland. "Better here than in the Channel!" Sighting a plowed field covered in new snow, he slid nose down and flipped to one side. It was when he tried to release his canopy that he found his left arm hanging useless and blood blurring his vision.

He passed out.

▲　▲　▲

Through a brain fog, Buzz registered voices. Pain from his arm and head confused him.

That's not English—French, not German. Are they arguing? Opening his eyes, he found he was lying on a bench in a church. A priest stood protectively in front of him, while a small, angry crowd gesticulated toward the door.

The sound of heavy boots silenced them all.

"Vas ist los hier?" Two Nazi officers shoved villagers aside to stand over Buzz. One nodded and said in German, "We saw your plane go down. The *Luftwaffe* will retrieve your plane, but the *Gestapo* has questions for you."

Fear wrapped itself around Buzz as he noted the lightning-and-skull insignias on the man's uniform. There was no need for him to understand German to realize what was in store.

Ignoring the priest's objections and the sanctuary of a church, the Nazi officer motioned for two of the townspeople to haul Buzz to his feet. He stumbled over the cobblestone streets, supported, none too gently, by the men. Sharp pain from his shoulder wound, where one of his escorts was gripping him, caused him to cry out. The man growled at him and thrust him forward. The throng barely avoided bumping into the Nazi officers, who halted abruptly at the steps to *Gestapo* headquarters. A *Luftwaffe* officer blocked the way.

After saluting, he smiled. "*Danke schoen* for bringing the prisoner this far. Because he is an American pilot, I believe he belongs to the *Luftwaffe* for interrogation . . . and treatment for his wounds." He motioned to a waiting vehicle.

The Nazi secret police scowled as they watched their prey driven off to the nearby airbase. Though half-conscious and understanding little, Buzz was relieved to see the backs of the *Gestapo*. He rubbed his knuckles and hoped luck was still with him. Then he breathed a prayer.

▲ ▲ ▲

German medics examined Buzz's injuries and gave him food and water before locking him in a cell. He slept, his dreams haunted by flying into the ground over and over. *Was his plane on fire?* He woke, his uniform damp with sweat despite the cold cell. An officer stood over him with a cup of hot coffee. Buzz managed to get upright and wrapped his frigid fingers around the mug.

"We talk now," the German translator said. 'What was your mission that brings you into France?"

All questioning failed, as Buzz gave only his name, rank, and serial number, as required by the Third Geneva Convention. Was his luck still holding, or would he face different types of interrogation? He shuddered at the thought.

▲ ▲ ▲

Days passed in pain and confusion, interrupted only by more questioning. His wounds received little attention. He was no longer in a cell but housed with other POWs. His arm hurt whenever he tried to use it; episodes of pain on the side of his head left him anxious and bewildered. Out in the exercise yard, he met other downed fliers, both American and English. A British medic checked Buzz every day, searching for signs of infection.

"Ya got some bloody nasty wounds there, Captain. I can't fix them, but I'll try to keep infection from setting in. The best I can hope for is to get them to heal over. Someone with more skill and tidier accommodations can do a right better job later on." He gave Buzz a knowing smile. "I suppose our German hosts offered you treatment and pain meds for information. Don't believe it. They keep what they have for their own guys. At times, I get some supplies through the Red Cross, but often the Germans have already pilfered from them. I do reserve whatever good stuff I get to help mates like you. You're bearing up well."

Weary, cold, and in pain, Buzz offered a weak smile. "Thanks, Doc."

CHAPTER 2

Laura Ann and I stood by her mailbox to chat a bit as she thumbed through the mail. "Oh, goody. I got a letter from Grandpa, Bobby. I hope he gets to join us soon."

I eyed the remodeling going on at her home. "How much longer do you figure?"

"It will be a while yet. Can you imagine? Grandpa thinks he might like to try living in the *mouse house*." She made a face. "And I can hardly wait to get out of it."

"Well, that trailer house might work for one person, instead of four, like you've had to do," I said. "Are German POWs still helping with construction?"

"Some, but as mom says, 'All in good time.' I'm not sure she has any idea that most of the carpenters are POWs.

Dad told me to be quiet about it." She put her finger to her lips and rolled her eyes. "Well, see you later, Bobby. Gotta go read what Grandpa wants me to write back in German this time." She waved the letter in the air. "You do know that he corrects what I write and sends it back to me, right?"

I laughed. "Studies at school and studies at home for you, Laura Ann. See you tomorrow."

It was neat how close Laura Ann was to her German-born grandpa. He'd immigrated about 50 years ago. I did look forward to meeting him. I glanced over at the ongoing construction at her house. Can't say I blamed her for itching to move out of that tiny trailer and into the new house. Her dad, though, was pretty clever adding that huge room last year so they could spread out more—with a bathroom, no less.

I slopped through the slush, crossed the street and headed up the hill. I kicked a rock ahead of me—then another, and another.

"Ouch!" A girl was rubbing the back of her calf as she frowned back at me.

"Oops, sorry." I smacked myself on the side of the head and loped up to where she was standing. "Afraid I wasn't paying attention."

"*Alles gut.* Uh, I-I am okay," she stammered.

"You must be new around here. My name is Bobby Bradley." I made a corny bow.

"I am Ruth Rosenblum. I move here from uh . . . England. I live up there." She pointed further up the hill. "Bye." And she was gone.

I turned down my street and grinned at the racket. Even from here I could hear Sarge rattling the gate. "Hey, boy, did you take care of Mom today?" I stooped to rub the German shepherd's ears, dodging his wet paws. "Wait till I get a towel to wipe your feet, and we'll go in."

It took a moment for my eyes to adjust after the bright sunlight. My Mom was sitting at the kitchen table, her hands twisting a handkerchief in her lap. A letter lay before her. She was crying.

"Mom, what's wrong?" But I already knew. It was Dad. Those unspoken fears that had hung over our heads for almost two years . . . what had happened?

She clenched my hand as I scooted a chair next to hers. "It's Dad, Bobby. He's missing in action . . . somewhere over France."

How could that be? He is supposed to only train pilots, not go on missions. I picked up the letter, and we read it together. *"We regret to inform you . . ."*

I hugged Mom close to me. She was trembling. "Mom, he's missing in action. He's not dead. I just won't believe that." I swallowed my own tears, trying to send the fear I felt with them. "Maybe his plane had trouble, but Dad is alive. He might be injured, or captured, but he's not dead, Mom. I have to believe that—and so do you. He is alive . . . somewhere."

Mom rested her head on my shoulder, wiped her eyes with one hand, and squeezed my hand with the other. "You're right, Bobby. We have to believe that . . . until we know otherwise." Her chin trembled as she nodded and managed a smile. "Yes, he's alive. Let's pray for Dad and for anyone who is helping him come home."

▲ ▲ ▲

The rest of the evening did not go well. Though we tried to cheer each other up by remembering happy times, that Fear, with a capital F, never left us. I talked her into going with me to walk Sarge, but our conversation was one-sided.

"I was really lucky to get Sarge, wasn't I, Mom?"

She nodded.

"Do you think Don's dad suggested that Major Jamison give him to me when he was transferred? Sarge was just an overgrown puppy then." I looked over at her.

"Yes, perhaps. He knew you would take good care of him." Mom's thoughts were far away, probably somewhere in France.

"He's good company for you while I'm at school, isn't he, Mom?"

"Yes, Bobby. I'm glad to have him." She gave me a woeful look. "But I'm tired. Let's go back."

Mom hugged me goodnight and went to her room. We'd forgotten about supper, so I made a couple of peanut butter and jelly sandwiches to share with Sarge. He'd eaten his own meal and now part of mine. I chuckled as I watched him work the peanut butter around in his mouth.

I let him out in the backyard and found a dry spot on the step to sit while he sniffed around. The old root cellar stood by the back fence, a silent reminder of our encounter with the Nazi spy. Had Laura Ann, Don, and I been stupid? Probably. The man was dangerous. It was hard to believe he lived in that attic bedroom of ours for several months and even ate with us. I wanted to tell Dad about it all. But Mom wouldn't let me write anything to him that might make him worry about us. It was important for him to concentrate on keeping himself safe. And now this!

My thoughts went to Dad. What happened over there? Where was he? Most important—was he safe and uninjured? I had so many things I wanted to tell him. I wanted him to meet Sarge and my friends; I wanted to tell him about Scouts and the scrap drives, and show him my airplane models. I could spend days filling him in.

I whistled for my dog, and we went inside. Gets dark early in January. I absently tapped a couple of my model planes hanging from the ceiling of my bedroom. Sarge curled on his rug, and I got ready for bed. Lying in the fading light, I named off each of the planes: P-51 Mustang, Lockheed P-35, P-47 Thunderbolt . . . . Which one did Dad fly? Shutting my eyes, I tried to visualize Dad. It was hard. I hadn't seen him in so long, except for the few photos he sent. I got up and went to my desk. Mom might be exhausted, but I was antsy.

Pulling out a tablet, I decided I would write about everything I wanted to tell him. It would help me to feel as if I were talking with him. I could save the letters and mail them to him when we learned where he was . . . maybe a prisoner-of-war camp . . hopefully a hospital if he's hurt. Perhaps the Red Cross could help get letters to him.

January 11, 1944
Dear Dad,

Mom and I got news today that you are MIA. We are both worried about you and miss you every day. It may be some time before you get to read this, but I need to write to you. It's been so long since I've been able to just talk to you. What? Almost a year and a half?

I try to imagine you over there in France. Was your plane shot down? Were you able to get away and hide? You aren't hurt, are you? I wish your answers would magically appear on this paper. Wouldn't that be neat if someone could invent that?

It is cold here, like it probably is in Europe this time of year. Are you warm enough? Is someone helping you? I heard there are groups of Resistance Fighters all over Europe. They risk their lives doing as much damage to the Nazis as they can. And, to rescue guys like you and keep you safe. I hope they are helping you right now. Mom is having a hard time with this news, but I try to keep her positive. We do believe you are alive and will come home.

I can hardly wait for you to meet my German shepherd dog. He really acts more pup than adult dog, as big as he is. His name is Sarge. When an officer was transferred, he gave him to me. Did you get the photo I sent? My friend Don took it. I think he is company for Mom while I'm at school. I mean Sarge, not my friend Don. Ha-ha! I am teaching Sarge to "come," "sit," and "stay." It's slow, as he would rather play, but he's smart and catching on.

I love you and miss you. Mom and I pray you are okay. I know you are alive and will come home when you can.

Love you, Dad

CHAPTER 3

PRISONER OF WAR
France

Which was worse—the cold, the pain, the hunger, or the nightmares? Rest escaped Buzz as images of his plane on fire and the ground rising to meet him invaded his sleep. Panic jolted him awake, or perhaps it was his own screams, as he'd dreamt of the Gestapo interrogating and beating him. Only when he could conjure the faces of Midge and Bobby in the darkness could he relax and feel the tension seep away. Into the frigid night he murmured, "I miss you. God willing, I will see you again."

Inside the POW compound building, the temperature varied little from outside. Buzz, wrapped in his blanket, gathered with others out in the exercise yard to soak up whatever warmth the winter sun offered. The men shared stories and photos, and traded addresses. They also shared a determination to survive this war and get home.

Several weeks passed. One day, Buzz sensed an undercurrent of excitement—or was it dread?—flowing through his companions. The medic came by.

"Hey, doc," he said, keeping his voice low. "What's going on? The guys seem edgy or excited."

"Over here, Captain. We can talk while I check your bandages. The guards seem a bit agitated, too. The scuttlebutt is that all air crews, which means most of us, will be moved into Germany. We'll still be prisoners of the German air force, nicknamed *Dulag Luft*. This transfer is a sort of a precaution for the Krauts."

"Why? What are they afraid of?"

The medic kept his head down to hide a grin. "We *are* in France—so the French Resistance, who else? Those chaps are getting bolder as they get better organized. I think they are now getting equipment drops from Mr. Churchill, too. The brave buggers are creating havoc with their sabotage as well as rescue missions. The *Luftwaffe* doesn't want any of us prize detainees to go missing."

"That's news to me. Think conditions will be any better in Germany?"

"I doubt it, Captain. Winter in Europe is the same everywhere," the medic answered. "Cold."

Buzz shook his head and winced. "I didn't know the Resistance was getting so strong. Good for them. Really dangerous business, I'm sure."

"It is." The medic gathered up his supplies. "But I'm really glad they're out there." He patted Buzz's shoulder. "Try not to shake your head. That has to hurt."

▲   ▲   ▲

Another nightmare brought Buzz into partial consciousness. Whispers lingered at the edge of wakefulness.

"We have to wait for no moon or heavy clouds."

Soft, but urgent, words continued in the darkness.

"Can't wait too long. I hear transports are on the way to collect the pilots."

"Who's on our list?"

"Only three. Percy Jones, Ian MacDonald, and maybe Andrews."

"What about Bradley? I doubt he'd survive transport for very long, especially in this cold and without better medical care for his wounds."

"Let's talk with the medic. He assures us Bradley is mobile."

Buzz moaned in his sleep and hugged his blanket tighter.

CHAPTER 4

Some News, at Last
Back in Utah

This past week had been super hard. Thoughts of Dad lingered on the edge of each moment I was in school. I rushed home—disappointed again. No word of where he was, how he was. I knew it was worse for Mom, alone every day, waiting for the mail, yet afraid to receive it.

Yesterday I saw evidence of where her every thought resided. I had commanded Sarge to "sit" before I unlatched the gate. He does try, but his tail wags so furiously, his rump scarcely touches down. I was laughing at him when I glanced at our front window. Something was different.

Then I saw it: the service flag. While I was at school, Mom had stitched a silver star over the blue service one. My Dad was not only serving—that silver star meant he'd been wounded or missing in action. I pray every day it's never gold.

I knew both Laura Ann's and Don's moms were good to visit my Mom over a cup of tea . . . coffee being so scarce. I'm glad they did. Yet, I imagined they went home wondering how Mom coped . . . and relieved it wasn't them. I saw the same reflected in Laura's and Don's faces myself.

As I latched the gate, I saw Mom watching from the door. I pointed to the service flag and gave her a thumbs up. She smiled as she let Sarge inside.

▲ ▲ ▲

Friday rolled around again. Again, I rushed home. Surprise! Mom was at the front door, a bit of a smile on her face and a letter in her hand.

"Bobby," she said as she drew me inside. "Remember Dad writing about his buddy Smitty? They flew together in Texas and now as wingmen. I knew him in Brownsville, but you were too young. Anyway, he wrote to us." She handed me the letter.

Dear Midge and Bobby,

I thought it might ease your worry a bit to know that Buzz may be wounded, captured, or even hiding out, but his plane did not go down in flames. That's every pilot's nightmare, you know. I was with him, testing equipment, when we ran into a couple Luftwaffe guys. His plane was hit and possibly crippled or losing fuel. I watched. There were no flames, and I saw no smoke. My guess is he was able to land it. He is a good pilot . . . one of the best.

Let's keep those good thoughts. If I hear any more scuttlebutt, I will let you know.

Smitty

Mom actually cooked a meal that evening, and we played a game of Monopoly.

▲ ▲ ▲

Saturday morning brought lots of new snow. I geared up and clipped the leash on Sarge to take him for a long walk. I stopped outside Don's house and whistled. He waved.

"Hey, come with us," I yelled. "We got a bit of news about Dad. Heard from his flying buddy."

A few minutes later, Don thumped down the front steps and patted Sarge's head. "I hope you got more information from his friend than the military provides its families." As his dad worked for the Office of Strategic Services— OSS (known as *Oh So Secret*)—Don was more aware of the workings—and shortcomings—of wartime operations than most kids.

We trudged up the hill to some open, snow-covered fields. I unclipped Sarge's leash to let him run free and nose around. "Yeah," I said. "We got a note from Dad's wingman Smitty. Mom knew him in Texas. He was flying with Dad when he went missing and figured we would be worried. So, he wrote what he knew. He said the last he saw of Dad's plane, it was not on fire, and he saw no smoke. That's the most important. Even if his plane was damaged, Smitty believed Dad probably crash-landed it somewhere. I just hope the Germans didn't track him and throw him in a POW camp." I cracked my knuckles and crossed my fingers. "But, most of all, that he's not wounded. It was a relief to receive just that bit of information."

Sarge bounded up with a stick and dropped it at my feet. "Go get it, Sarge!" I threw it across the field and watched my dog bound through the snow. "Next time, I'll bring your ball—the red one—so we can find it in the snow."

We stood and talked, taking turns throwing the stick for Sarge. Don, who played baseball, pitched low and fast. I'm taller, so I threw the stick high so Sarge had to leap to retrieve it mid-air. We kept him busy.

After a time, I whistled, and Sarge returned, panting, his tongue dripping saliva. I clipped the leash on. "Let's go the long way 'round to let Sarge cool down."

Don patted the dog's heaving flanks. "If my mom wasn't allergic to dog fur, I'd ask for a dog myself. Sarge is a really nice dog. You were lucky to get him, Bob."

"Yeah, I was. I sometimes think about Captain Jamison. I wonder where he is and if he misses Sarge." I elbowed Don. "And I don't mind sharing, you know."

▲ ▲ ▲

That evening Mom was listening to music on the radio and doing some mending, so I went to my room to write more to Dad.

Hi Dad,

> *Things are not quite so gloomy here tonight. We still miss you and worry about you, but getting a note from your buddy Smitty helped. He said he tracked your plane as you went down. He saw no fire or smoke. I guess all pilots dread that, as it makes them so helpless. He wanted to reassure us. He said you were a skillful pilot and doubtless managed a crash landing.*
>
> *I just didn't feel quite so alone after reading his letter. I hope he keeps in touch. Mom seems relieved, too.*
>
> *Love you lots. So does Sarge, though he doesn't know it yet.*

▲ ▲ ▲

A week later, another storm arrived, plus a short note from Smitty. He had no more news—only encouragement and a promise to stay in touch.

Don and I took Sarge out again. My dog was growing fast, delighting in bounding through the drifts. Then he caught sight of a rabbit and took chase. I whistled for him without success, and finally went to find him. He was digging furiously in a snowbank.

I clipped on his leash and made him sit. After getting his attention, I scolded him.

"He's just doing what dogs do, I 'spect," Don said. "We'll have to make sure we spot the rabbits before Sarge does."

We turned down the hill toward home when I saw a girl out in her yard. I waved, and she waved back.

"Who's that?" Don said. "I haven't seen her at school."

"Her name is Ruth something or other. I forget. Met her some time back, walking home. Actually, I hit her with a rock I was kicking." Don gave me a questioning look. I shrugged my shoulders. "She said she's from England. I think she's younger than us."

CHAPTER 5

Cold, Dark, and Dangerous

France

It was a moonless night. Shadowy figures crept through the barracks. Buzz startled as a hand covered his mouth. Someone touched his shoulder, urging him to get up. Head pain fogged his thinking as he was helped from his cot.

"Quiet, Captain. Take your time. Are you okay standing?" Buzz nodded as he clutched his blanket to him. "See the open door? Wait there."

Buzz stood a moment to get fully awake. He quietly made his way to the door. Soft snores and mumbling rose from the cots around him. *What was going on? Why had he been awakened and no one else?*

He reached the doorway. The body of a guard rested just inside . . . unconscious or dead? The outer yard glowed bright as day as the searchlight made its sweep. He found two others huddled in the dark doorway. Blackness returned as the searchlight swept to the far side of the exercise yard. Three figures scurried across and slipped inside to join them.

A voice whispered in a strong French accent, "Two at a time. Wait for the darkness. Stay low. We guide you. You first, MacDonald. Bradley, you with Pierre."

By turn, they scuttled spiderlike in the dark and crawled through a breach in the barbed-wire fence; then they flattened themselves in a ditch. Time seemed to stand still as each pair sprinted across. A French voice whispered in Buzz's ear, "Good job. Lie quiet. We wait, then crawl."

The January cold seeped through Buzz's uniform and made his arm ache. He clenched his jaw to remain silent. Timing their movements to the rhythm of the blinding searchlight, they edged into the far brush. Hunched over, they followed a trail to a pickup point and clambered into a horse-drawn hay wagon. Buzz released a small cry of pain and passed out.

▲ ▲ ▲

A rosy dawn tinted the snow. Wood smoke drifted from a low chimney. Three airmen, wrapped in blankets, sipped hot tea before the fire. Their rescuers stood around, chatting in French with the farm couple.

"How are you doing, mate?" the airman next to Buzz said. "Big surprise for you, I'm sure. We didn't dare tell you for fear you might talk in your sleep. You did jolly well, though."

By now Buzz understood the French Resistance had smuggled him and his companions out of the POW camp. "Why me? I'll only slow everyone down." He sipped his tea. "Not that I'm not glad to be with you."

"Our camp medic wasn't sure you would survive the transport into Germany, scheduled for next week. Your wounds need attention, but you can walk. He insisted you join us. These chaps," he motioned to their guides, "do the best they can for us. They hate the bloody Nazis with a passion. It's dangerous for them, but they feel they are evening the score a bit. They are a brave lot."

"I don't understand much French," Buzz said. "Have you any idea what happens next? Do we stay here for now?"

"Not likely. The Germans are probably searching for us right this minute. Eat your bread and cheese. I think we're going on another hayride."

▲ ▲ ▲

For the next week, Buzz and his two companions were shuffled from one safe house to another, always with different guides. Huddling in a frigid barn one evening, the three looked forward to the hot soup promised by the farm wife. She arrived, accompanied by a local doctor. As he checked each airman, he apologized for the lack of medical care. He tucked a few pain pills into Buzz's pocket.

"Perhaps these will be enough to get you across the Channel to better treatment. Already you smell the salty air, *oui*?" With an encouraging smile, he added, "It won't be long now. Good luck." Buzz thanked him and felt the urge to tap his knuckles.

New guides slipped in, followed by three strangers, one a woman. "Meet your fellow sailors, *non*? These three have been brave, what we call *helpers*, but now they need safety for themselves. They join you to avoid the SS. I'll let you know. Be ready." He disappeared as if a ghost.

▲ ▲ ▲

Two nights later, a voice whispered to the six fugitives, "Time to go. Leave nothing behind. Storm clouds are blocking the moon. We go quick."

Exhausted and in pain, Buzz struggled to keep up. Grasping a rope to stay in line, the troupe stumbled across a rocky area for some distance. They paused atop a cliff and looked down on the beach and the restless waves of the English Channel. "We are in Brittany. That is Bonaparte Beach down there. Be careful—the trail is steep and rocky. We don't want to lose any of you now."

A biting wind carried the salty tang of open water to Buzz's tongue. The path was treacherous, the night dark, the sea a roiling blackness. He inched his feet along, conscious of someone nearby guiding him. Uniforms proved no match for the deep chill of the sea. Two rowboats creaked as they rocked offshore. The woman and Buzz were the first to climb aboard.

"Keep low," a sailor admonished. "A British gunboat is waiting for you out there.

Another sailor glanced up at the covering storm and added, "Let's hope the German planes aren't patrolling on a night like this."

It was colder yet on the sea, and Buzz shivered in a thin blanket. *Would they never reach the waiting British gunboat? My head hurts, my arm aches. I'm so cold.* At last, strong arms hoisted him and the others onboard. Dry blankets and waterproof covers replaced the soaked ones. Buzz was handed a drink, lukewarm but satisfying. He slept.

CHAPTER 6

Safe at Last
English Channel

It was hours before the silver edge of the moon peeked through the storm clouds. The boat, though tossed about in the choppy waters, chugged toward England. Fear of pursuit and discovery, of being betrayed, gripped the tiny troupe of travelers. The pain, the cold, and the daily tension of trying to keep up, to not be a burden exhausted Buzz. Now he slept, too worn down to feel fear, barely aware of the sound of enemy planes above searching the waves below.

Rapid gunfire startled him awake. A voice cautioned, "Stay down. They haven't discovered us. Just hoping we'll respond."

Buzz repositioned himself and dozed as the buzzing of German planes faded. Reduced engine beat and calmer waters caused him to stir. Loud voices guided the vessel into place, followed by the grating of a ramp connecting boat to land. He was safe and smiled for the first time in weeks as an ambulance delivered him to a hospital.

Comforting hands cleaned his body; skillful fingers probed his wounds; warm soup soothed his throat and eased the hunger pangs. Buzz slept.

▲ ▲ ▲

Much later, a voice brought him to consciousness. "Captain Bradley, can you hear me?"

A pillow was propping his head up, and he opened his eyes. "Where am I? Who are you?"

"It's okay. You're safe now and in hospital in Plymouth, England," a white-coated man said. "I'm Dr. Hugh Abbott. You've had quite an adventure—and a 24-hour nap." He pulled a chair to the bedside and smiled at Buzz. "Are you up for a bit of a chat?" He motioned for a nurse to leave a tray.

Buzz's eyes refused to focus. He nodded at the doctor. "I can't think straight. Everything is all jumbled together. My plane went down . . . the Gestapo . . . then a POW camp with other fliers." He touched his head gingerly. "I was wounded." Taking a quick breath, he went on. "Then I escaped with others . . . the French hid us in wagons, barns . . . lots of French people I couldn't understand." He shook his head, winced, and grinned. "I do know *not* to do that."

"Slow down, Captain. You'll sort it over time." The doctor placed the soup on a tray in front of him. "You work on that soup while I check your injuries. We need to put some weight on you. Obviously, the Germans did not share their *Wiener schnitzel* and *Kuchen* with their prisoners. You'll be here for a time. Then you're going home, and I hope surgeons there can help you more." He motioned the nurse back. "And, this young lady is going to write a letter for you to your family. They need to know you are safe. I'll check back tomorrow." He stood to leave and pointed. "Finish that soup. That's an order."

Buzz felt his whole being relax. Midge, Bobby, Home. The tension in his neck and shoulders released. He closed his eyes and the tightness across his forehead, around his eyes, and in his jaw evaporated into a sense of peace.

"Sir, would you like to dictate a letter now, or shall I come back later?"

Buzz squinted at her name tag. "No, Alice. Now. Please. It's been so long since I've been in touch. Can you write while I finish this soup and talk? You probably spell a lot better than I do." He grinned at his own small joke. It felt so good.

Half an hour later, Buzz gave his home address to Nurse Alice and requested that his buddy Smitty be notified of his rescue.

▲ ▲ ▲

For a week, Buzz rested, ate, and gained strength. However, the pain in his arm and continuous headache remained. Nightmares returned, along with confusion.

One afternoon, he woke from a nap to find a military figure standing over him. "Captain Bradley. I need to ask you some questions. Are you up for that?" The man shook Buzz's hand and sat down. "You can call me 'Jason.'"

Buzz nodded his head and was immediately sorry he had. *This must be my debriefing. What if I can't remember or get things confused?*

"Head still bothers you, eh? Relax and just tell me what you can. I can match it with what your two companions on the Shelburne Line have reported. We are hoping to keep that escape route open as long as we can." He looked over his glasses at Buzz. "Of course, this is not something you write home about, you know."

Jason asked questions, made notes, and showed Buzz a map.

"The only place I know for sure, Sir, is where my plane went down and that there was an airfield close by. After that, I wouldn't swear to anything."

After a time, the man stood, thanked Buzz for the information, and left the room. Buzz shook his head, gently. *I wonder how much of my letter home was censored.*

CHAPTER 7

Best News Yet

Back in Utah

I spied Don at our front gate as I pulled down the earflaps of my aviator cap, blew Mom a kiss, and patted Sarge's head. "Be good, you two. Take care of each other."

If it hadn't been so slippery, I might have skipped down the walk. "Great news, Don! We got a letter from Dad. He's safe, and he's coming home."

Don cheered and gave me a "thumbs up" with one hand and a "V for victory" with the other. "Wow! When did you hear? Is he okay?"

"Got the letter yesterday. He's been in a hospital in England. A nurse wrote the letter for him. He's been wounded," I croaked out those last words. "But he's alive. That's what counts. Some of his letter was blacked out, but he will be stateside before long. We learned there's a military hospital in Brigham City, so we can go see him." As I latched the gate, I leaned over and ruffled my dog's ears. "You'll meet Dad before long, Sarge. He's gonna love you."

We skated down the hill through the snow to meet Laura Ann at the corner. I just felt giddy. They let me jabber on as I shared the news with her, and then over again. My chest felt as if it might burst. I was going to see my Dad again. When? It couldn't be soon enough. "I'm so happy today, I won't even mind having Arnie in my woodshop class again this semester."

Laura Ann frowned. "Not many kids like him. Not even the guys. He's so loud and pushy."

"Yeah, he can be a bully. I was up against him in JV football," Don said. "He thinks he's varsity material already and lets everyone know it."

"Well, he is not ruining my day today." I threw a snowball at a telephone pole. "Not even Arnie!"

▲ ▲ ▲

Last period, I opened my locker in the hall outside the basement woodshop classroom to stow things away for the weekend. I had to come up with a semester project. *What would Mom like?*

Arnie rumbled by, banged his locker door open, and announced to anyone listening, "I know what I'm building . . . a gun rack for my bedroom."

"Come on, Arnie. What are you going to use it for?" Jay, an upper classman, taunted. "You don't have a rifle. Don't even know how to use one."

"I do so," Arnie bragged. "I sneak my dad's .22 sometimes when he's out on the road. Shoot it in that big empty field." Arnie jutted out his chin. "When he sees how good I am, maybe he will give it to me."

"You be careful," Jay said. "Even a .22 is dangerous. If the cops, or worse yet, your dad catches you, you'll be in big trouble."

"Who asked you?" Arnie said and slammed his locker shut.

I shuddered at the thought of him with a firearm. Even a slingshot!

▲ ▲ ▲

Mom met me at the door, her eyes bright and a smile on her face. "Guess what? We've been invited to dinner at the McDowells' tonight. They want to know all about Dad's rescue, or as much as we know. Talking about seeing him again makes it more real. Get yourself tidied up."

An hour later, we knocked on the McDowells' door.

"Thanks so much for inviting us," Mom said. "I am so excited; I just have to share our news."

"We are truly happy for you," Angie McDowell said. "Tell us about it over dinner. It's about ready. Hope you like venison."

Talk bounced back and forth across the table. Mom fairly glowed with joy. The evening passed quickly. I did notice that Major McDowell listened but didn't say much . . . until we were about to leave. "Midge, let me know as soon as you learn when Buzz is expected at Bushnell General Hospital in Brigham City. It's a 25-mile drive up there. We have people going back and forth all the time. Maybe we can work out some transportation to help you families."

"Oh, Brian, what a help that would be," Mom said. "Thanks so much. I can hardly wait to see Buzz."

As Mom and I strolled over to our house, our spirits were lighter than over the past two years. Before bedtime, I wrote Dad again. There wouldn't be time to mail it, but I just had to talk with him.

Dear Dad,

Mom and I got your letter today. We both feel as if we are floating on air and so happy and thankful that you are safe. We have no idea what you have been through but can barely wait to see you again—in person! Just to touch you and see your eyes on us. I have missed you for so long but only right now realize just how much.

I hope you have a safe flight home. We will get to the hospital to see you as soon as we can.

Love, Bobby

CHAPTER 8

Where's Sarge?

Saturday morning, I let Sarge out. He buried his nose in the snow and raced about the yard. I laughed as he rolled and played. He was young but close to full-size. "Be back in a bit to feed you, Sarge. Stop playing, and go do your business."

I went inside to enjoy breakfast with Mom. We were counting the days until we could see Dad, although we had no idea when that would be. Still, we enjoyed the anticipation. Relief and happiness had moved into our house as fear moved out.

"I knew Dad was alive, Mom." I blew on the spoonful of hot oatmeal. "I just knew he was."

"I know you did, Bobby." She patted my hand. "Now, help me get things done around here so we are free to visit your Dad when he is back."

"Okay, Mom. Let me feed Sarge first." I opened the front door and whistled. I called, "Hey, fellow, chow time."

No dog.

I froze at the sight. The gate was standing open. Sarge was nowhere to be seen. Lightheaded, I clutched the door frame as my knees threatened to crumple. The familiar fear and dread gripped me. I shook my head to clear my thinking and raced into the street. I yelled his name, surveying the neighborhood for any sign of my dog. I ran back inside for a coat, cap, and boots. "Mom, Sarge is gone. I have to go find him. He couldn't have gone too far." Running to Don's front step, I yelled. "Don, I need help. Sarge is missing."

Within minutes, we were searching the surrounding area. "Sarge, come." Whistle and whistle. "Come, boy. Come here." We scoured for blocks around, peeking over fences and checking vacant lots. I kept hoping to see that tail of his wagging behind a shrub. Hours later, exhausted and afraid, I returned home, hoping to find him there.

No dog.

"Take a break, Bobby," Mom said. "Have a quick sandwich and a glass of milk. Maybe he will show up."

Distraught, I felt like when we learned Dad was MIA. Now it was Sarge. "Mom, what if someone took him? He's a really nice-looking dog. Maybe he followed someone and is lost. Do you think he can find his way home?" I wolfed down the sandwich and gulped the milk. "I have to go find him." I slammed the door.

It was getting dark when I lumbered home, cold, wet, exhausted, and hoarse. "I didn't find him, Mom." I couldn't hold back tears. "I was so happy about Dad coming home. I could hardly wait for him to see Sarge. What if he doesn't come home?"

Mom held me as my shoulders shook with sobs. "We'll go to church tomorrow. Perhaps someone saw Sarge. I'm sure others will help you look. And, we'll ask for prayer for his safe return." She smiled into my blubbery face. "They were answered for Dad, weren't they?"

She was right, but it was little comfort as I stumbled to my bedroom. The sight of Sarge's blanket brought tears to my eyes and a lump the size of a bomb waited to explode in my throat. My thoughts reached out to my dog. *Sarge, where are you? It's so cold at night. Did you find a place to sleep? You aren't hurt, are you? Please come home! Be waiting on the front step. I left the gate open for you.* I wiped at my eyes. *No! Better yet, bark your head off. I'll hear you.*

All night long, I imagined or dreamed Sarge was hurt, lost, hungry, cold. Every scenario was worse than the last. The rug he slept on haunted me. He should be there, curled up, with his chin on his paws. When I dozed off, I imagined him scratching at the door, whining to come in. It was so real that, twice, I got up to go look. Where was my dog?

At a loss, I grabbed his blanket and held it tightly, burying my nose in his doggy smell. Fur made me sneeze and got in my eyes but couldn't get past the tears and snotty nose. I flopped into the chair at my desk and fumbled for a pencil and Dad's letter.

Dad. I wish you were here. My dog is missing, and I'm so afraid. It's like when we got your MIA letter. So helpless. I want to do something, but I don't know what. I'm exhausted but I doubt I will sleep.

▲ ▲ ▲

Sunday morning, I woke up all tangled up in Sarge's blanket and ran to the door to see if he had come home. No dog. I dressed and slurped down a bowl of cereal; then I went outside to do a quick search before Laura Ann's family picked us up for church.

Mom was right. Eight people offered to help search. Laura Ann joined me and Don. "I brought some treats for others to coax Sarge home. He's probably hungry."

Even with the extra help, night came with no sign of Sarge. I could barely hold it together. "Mom, what if he's locked up someplace and can't come home?"

▲ ▲ ▲

I begged to stay home from school to search for my dog, but Mom was firm. "Laura Ann's mom has their car and called to offer to drive me to look for him, Bobby. You will be missing some school, I imagine, when Dad is home. Go today. If he's not home by this evening, you can take tomorrow to look some more."

I went to school, but it seemed as if the final bell would never ring. Don met me on the front steps. "Let's walk the long way around. Maybe we'll find him."

I nodded. Where could Sarge have disappeared to? We searched up and down the streets, checked the alleys, and peered over fences. Darkness came, but no dog.

Tuesday was a repeat of Saturday, Sunday, and Monday. Sarge couldn't have just disappeared into thin air. I was sure someone was keeping him locked up . . . or he would come home.

Dusk was falling as Don and I dragged ourselves toward my house. "Who's that at your door talking to your mom?"

I squinted. My eyes burned so badly from the snow; and, also, from crying, big as I am. "Can't tell from here. Hope it's not bad news. I don't see Sarge in the yard."

We hurried to the gate and stood stock still at the sight of the visitor. "Hi, boys," Mom said. "Have you met Ruth? She lives a couple streets up. Come see what she brought." She was beaming.

I caught sight of a wagging tail inside, rushed past Ruth and Mom, and fell to my knees. "Sarge! Where have you been, boy? I looked . . ." Then I noticed the bandages.

Mom ushered both Ruth and Don inside. "Ruth has a story to tell, Bobby. All of you sit down. I'll get some refreshments."

Sarge licked my hand as his tail thumped the floor. I scratched his ears and leaned down to kiss his head. "Where did you find him, Ruth? The bandages? What happened?"

Ruth clasped her hands together and looked down at the dog. "I saw you two with the dog that one day, so I knew he was yours. Last Saturday morning, I was scraping snow off the step when I heard a loud pop. I have heard that sound before—back home—so I knew what it was." She paused, as though remembering, and, then continued. "I listened, but nothing. I was finishing our walk when I saw something. At first I *hat nicht kennt*, uh, do not know—but I saw a dog limping. It is yours, I think." She nodded at Sarge. "I called for my father to come with me. He looked at where the dog is hurt. He is a doctor, you know."

This was news to us. "Wow! You are one lucky pup, buddy." I continued ruffling my dog's ears. "You said that was Saturday?"

Ruth continued. "Yes. My father carried your dog to our house, where he could tend the wound. He was shot, you know."

"Shot!" Don said. "Who would do such a thing?"

I clenched my jaw. *I think I know.*

"My Papa made Sarge sleep while he removed the bullet and bandaged him. He said he needed to be quiet for a couple days while we care for him." Ruth smiled. "But he limped to the door, scratched, and whined all day today. I did not know where you lived, but he did. So, he brought me with him." The girl shrugged and reached to pet the shepherd. Sarge was now asleep, with his head on my knee.

"We are so grateful to you and your father, Ruth," Mom said. "You were an answer to our prayers." She sent a *Didn't-I-tell-you-so?* glance my way. "If there is any way we can repay or help you, don't hesitate to say so."

Don and Ruth left the house quietly. I stayed on the floor with Sarge. *I'll get even with you, Arnie. You'll pay for shooting my dog.*

Mom was watching me. "I can see you think you know who shot Sarge, Bobby. Let that go, and tend to Sarge. Our prayers were answered. Be thankful." She brought me a pillow and blanket. "I know you aren't going to leave him. Get some sleep."

As I stroked Sarge's fur, I tried to imagine what had happened. Did Sarge jump at the gate, unlatching it himself, to follow another dog? I could fix that. Maybe he went back up to the field, hoping to chase more rabbits. Someone, maybe Arnie, was out with a gun. Did that person shoot at my dog on purpose?

And Ruth. What did she mean when she said she'd heard that pop before, *back* home? In England? But she knew what to do and got help. When Sarge is better, I'll walk him to her house to thank her father for taking care of him.

My heart was still thumping to the beat of Sarge's tail. I was relieved, but I was angry, too. I promised myself I would find out if Arnie had done this. What I would do about it, I didn't know. Not yet. I'd talk to Dad. I tiptoed to my room to retrieve my tablet.

Dear Dad,

Except for learning you were MIA, I've not had worse days than the past four. Sarge went missing. Lots of people helped me look for him but no dog. I imagined all sorts of things: he ran off, although I knew he wouldn't; he was stolen; he wandered off and couldn't find his way home. But I never imagined he had been shot!

Ruth, a new girl whose dad is a doctor, found him. He was wounded. Shot, of all things! They took him home and her dad removed the bullet and patched him up. So, all the time I was searching for Sarge, he was at their house. And Sarge guided her to bring him home today.

I'm so glad he is okay or will be—like you. But, Dad, I'm so angry. I think I know who shot him, and I don't know what to do about it. I'm sure it's a kid in my woodshop class. He's been bragging about sneaking out with his dad's .22. He's a big bully of a guy.

I'll wait. He's bound to say something sooner or later. He likes to brag. What do I do then? No telling what he'll do if he's challenged. But, I can't do nothing. He hurt my dog! When you're well again, maybe you can tell me what to do.

I am so happy to have him home safe. Sarge and I are having a sleepover on the living room carpet tonight.

Love, Bobby

CHAPTER 9

I secured the rope to keep the gate closed. "Can't have you taking yourself for a walk anymore, Sarge." The dog gingerly limped down the walk, though nothing hindered the tail wag. "Maybe we'll go for a short walk after school." I waved to Mom, who was standing in the doorway.

Don joined me, and we trotted down the hill to meet Laura Ann. "I bet you were relieved to get Sarge back home, Bobby. Thanks for calling to let me know." She elbowed me. "Who's this girl, Ruth? I'd like to meet her."

"Well, yeah. I'm sure she would be happy to meet you, too. I don't think she knows many girls. Don't know much about her myself, but I'm glad I hit her with a rock."

"You did what?" Laura Ann stopped and stared at me.

"It was an accident." I shrugged my shoulders. "You know me and my kicking rocks. I apologized. I wonder what she does all week. I haven't noticed her at school."

▲ ▲ ▲

Arnie was a different matter. His voice carried through the basement hallway outside woodshop class as he slapped a buddy on the back. "Yeah, great weekend. Dad was on the road again, so I had fun with his rifle. I even measured the .22 so I make my gun rack the right size." He elbowed his way into class.

I usually avoided sitting anywhere near Arnie, as he was so obnoxious. Now, I wanted to be close enough to hear what he was shooting at. He was bound to brag more about the .22.

Mr. Swanson called the class to order, and he handed out large sheets of drawing paper. "Okay, fellas, use this paper to sketch out your semester project. Think how it's going to fit together . . . corners, angles. Will it hang on a wall, a hook, a stand? Outside or inside? On the other side of the paper, draw each section, and add the measurements. I'll come around and talk with each of you."

I thought about a birdhouse for Mom. Where would she put it? Someplace where cats couldn't reach it. I went to the resource shelf to look for ideas and passed by Arnie's bench.

"So, what are you thinking of building, Arnie?" Mr. Swanson said.

"I want to build a gun rack . . . uh . . . for my dad. He lets me take his .22 out all the time to go shoot," Arnie lied.

I caught the doubtful look on Mr. Swanson's face. "You're not old enough to shoot on your own, Arnie. Doesn't he have his firearms locked up? Why would he need a gun rack?"

"Oh, he doesn't lock it up. He wraps it in a blanket and keeps it under his bed. I'm sure he'd like a rack for . . . uh, his bedroom wall."

I stood, thumbing through magazines. *You are such a liar, Arnie. If I find out you're targeting animals, and especially dogs, you're in big trouble.*

I took several magazines back to my bench and found a neat birdhouse to build. Mr. Swanson stopped with suggestions. "That's a good project, Bobby, with spring on the way." He turned to look at Arnie. "You might consider something like this. Maybe your mom would appreciate one? It'll be Mother's Day in a few months."

Arnie grunted back. I felt his angry glare.

A few minutes before dismissal, the teacher had us pack up our plans. "Class, I'm sure some of you may have projects you've done on your own at home. Bring in whatever you have—stools, shelves, toys, models. Each day, we'll take time for you to do a bit of 'Kindergarten show-and-tell.'" He grinned. "I think we may have some hidden creativity among you. I'm looking forward to seeing what you have."

At the lockers, Arnie's voice echoed in the hall. "I know what I'm bringing, but it's a secret. All of you will want to know how I made it." He banged his locker door. "It's so cool."

CHAPTER 10

Show-and-Tell

I had not realized that joy was a real thing, a feeling that stays with you, no matter what you're doing. But, it is. Waiting for Dad to arrive at the military hospital and seeing him again filled every thought. Mom stayed busy with all her preparations, and I needed to get her birdhouse underway. Chores weren't chores with something great to look forward to.

Today I was taking in one of my model planes for our shop *show-and-tell*. I picked one of the fighter planes and packed it in tissue paper and then in a large paper bag. Made of balsa wood and tissue paper, the planes were pretty delicate. I guess I looked forward to showing off a bit. I did a good job on them, even if I do say so myself.

I remembered the first one I did, with Dad's help before he went off to war. I was about twelve or so, I think. I made a lot of mistakes, and we laughed at my clumsy work. Then he left. I continued to find kits of different planes. I guess it kept me feeling he was there with me. I had about a dozen flying above my bed now. I could hardly wait for Dad to see them.

I waved goodbye to Mom and Sarge, and I walked to school with my friends. I secured my plane in my locker for last-period shop class.

Concentrating on school assignments seemed a lost cause. The only thing on my mind was seeing Dad again. Finally, it was my end-of-the-day shop class, and I retrieved the sack from my locker. Arnie had a large bag under his arm and a huge grin on his face. No surprise there.

Mr. Swanson decided to start class with our show-and-tell, probably because Arnie kept rattling his paper bag. "Okay, Arnie," he said. "Show us what you have in that sack."

Arnie reached into the bag and pulled out something in the shape of a gun with a long barrel, but quite crude. "This," he announced, "is my rubber gun. I made it myself, and it works great." He waved about a wooden gun with a spring-type clothespin taped to the back of the handle. "And here is the ammunition." He pulled out rubber strips cut from an inner tube with a knot tied in the center of each. "This is how I load it. It stings a bit." He laughed. "Just ask my sister.

"Only takes a minute." He clipped one end of a rubber strip into the clothespin and stretched the other end over the barrel. He aimed it at different classmates and settled on me.

The class was silent; even Mr. Swanson was immobile.

Jay acted, knocking Arnie's weapon out of his hand. "What's wrong with you, Arnie? That is not an inside toy. It's not a toy at all."

The clothespin released its *rubber bullet,* which slapped into the heater under the window. Arnie's face flushed with anger. He turned on Jay. "What'd ya go and do that for? I shoulda aimed it at you."

Mr. Swanson defused the situation and helped Arnie *save face* by asking where he got his idea and how he made the gun. "Probably not the best item to have in school, though, Arnie. The principal might take it away from you." He insisted the contraption go back in the sack before turning to me. "So, Bobby, I see you brought something also. Will you show us?"

I stood and carefully unwrapped my model plane. Lots of the guys oohed and aahed when they saw it. "I make model airplanes. My dad is a pilot in the war . . . or he was." I blinked hard so I could continue. "He was shot down but is coming home next week." I hadn't meant to tell about Dad. It just came out. "I've built about a dozen planes, and they hang from the ceiling of my bedroom. Dad was never able to tell us what he flew . . . so I made all I could find."

Mr. Swanson examined the plane. "You've done some really careful work here, Bobby. Your birdhouse should look spectacular."

Arnie huffed and pouted the rest of the period.

The bell was about to ring, so I gathered tissue to rewrap my plane. Arnie lumbered by and bumped my arm. My plane fell. His boot crushed one wing. "Oops, sorry." He busted out the door, a satisfied smirk on his face.

Jay was enraged; Mr. Swanson tried not to be.

I wrapped the pieces. "I'm sure I can repair the wing . . . might be a different color."

▲ ▲ ▲

I was glad not to run into Arnie the next day. I wasn't sure just how to handle him. Should I confront him, ignore him, or what? I wished my Dad were there to talk to. Woodshop class was underway when Arnie slipped in and sat at the back of the room. Mr. Swanson nodded at him. "Don't forget to take your cap off."

We all turned to look his way and gasped. All, that is, except Jay. Arnie's eye was bruised, his lip cut, his face red and swollen in places. Had whatever happened to him taught him anything? Or, would it make him worse? Was it even related to what had happened in class?

After class, I approached Jay in the hallway. "Uh, Jay, do you have any idea what happened to Arnie?"

"Well, it wasn't any of the guys. I do know that," Jay said.

"He looks pretty rough. I don't want it to be because of me or anything," I said with a shrug. "He looks like someone took him to task."

"Can't say for sure, Bobby, but I live in his neighborhood. Arnie's dad is a big fellow. He hauls stuff over the road . . . war items, I guess. He's not home a lot, but you can hear him when he is. Loud voice, big temper. Maybe Arnie got crosswise with his dad again." Jay tossed his hair out of his eyes. "I know Arnie can be obnoxious, but sometimes I feel sorry for him. I think the dad favors the sister, Donna. She's a super student, and Arnie is . . . uh . . . just Arnie."

"Well, thanks, Jay," I said. "I didn't know that about the family."

We walked down the hall together. Jay turned to me and touched my sleeve. "I'm so glad your dad is safe, Bobby. I hope he's home soon."

"Thanks, Jay. And, for telling me about Arnie and his family." I wasn't going to waste any time dwelling on that family. I was going to see my Dad this Sunday.

CHAPTER 11

PLYMOUTH, ENGLAND, TO UTAH

Back in England

Buzz maneuvered himself into a wheelchair, grimacing at the pain in his left arm. He was holding his head, a wave of dizziness flowing over him as he was wheeled toward an exit.

Dr. Hugh Abbott walked beside him. "I am recommending immediate surgery on that shoulder, Captain Bradley. I could schedule it here, but that would delay your return to the States." The doctor touched his arm. "I know you are eager to see your family as soon as possible. You do know that the military hospital for the Rocky Mountain region is not far from your home. It'll be easier to get to see your family. Won't be long now." He squeezed a shoulder, the right one. "And, the best of luck, Sir."

Buzz shook the doctor's hand. "I'm so banged up . . . not at all like they last saw me. Seems ages ago now. But I'm mighty eager to see them. Thanks for your care here."

The doctor handed Buzz his medical file plus some pain pills, and a nurse wheeled him to his waiting transport.

▲ ▲ ▲

The flight was long and tedious, with intermittent stopovers. Buzz tried to sleep but woke disoriented or perspiring from nightmares. Medication helped the pain but added to his confusion. He lost track of time and place.

Someone tapped his shoulder. "Captain Bradley, we are about to land at Hill Air Base. Welcome home." A young woman in some sort of uniform smiled down at him. "My name is Corporal Patricia Hunt. I'll help you off this plane and onto a military transport to drive you to the hospital in Brigham City. It's only 30 miles. You're almost home. They will take good care of you there." She stooped down to look into Buzz's eyes. "And thank you for all you've done and been through."

Still a bit foggy, Buzz winced as he shook his head. "Wow, from one side of the world to the other. I choose America any day." He grinned. "Thanks for the lift."

▲ ▲ ▲

A few hours later, Buzz found himself in a hospital bed, thinking clearly but in more pain. A nurse brought in fresh water. A doctor strode in with a file in his hands.

"Hello, Captain Bradley. You have endured quite a journey these past few weeks for someone with your injuries."

He grabbed a chair. Buzz felt his intent stare. "You have had enough adventure for one man. I would like to hear what you are able to tell, but, first, will you allow me to examine your wounds? My name is Isaac Rosenblum. I am a surgeon, so perhaps I can help you."

Using his good right arm, Buzz tried to wrestle himself into a more upright position. "I could use some help, Doctor. My left arm is useless except as a source of pain."

"And it's hurting you quite badly right now, I think." The doctor peered over his tiny wire-framed glasses. "I cut your pain meds to do this evaluation. But I will up them again."

After pressing and poking, scribbling notes as he went, Dr. Rosenblum leaned back in his chair. "Although your skin has healed over, you still have shrapnel in your shoulder that, I think, is pressing on a nerve or two. This bone was cracked," he pointed where, "but not broken and has healed on its own. If you will allow me, I would like to schedule surgery to remove the metal." He waited for Buzz's response.

"I'm no good like this, Doctor. They said at the hospital in Plymouth that I was lucky I had no infection. I credit that to the British medic in the POW camp. He tended me every day." Buzz's eyes glistened at the memory. "My wife and son are visiting tomorrow. I can't wait to see them. Will you be here then?"

"Not this weekend, but I'm not through with you yet. We haven't talked about those headaches and nightmares. Tell me what happened to you over there."

Buzz told about his flying with Smitty, and being shot down and captured. "The worst was that I was always so cold and tired. I had a hard time getting much sleep due to the pain and nightmares. I get dizzy, and it hurts when I nod or shake my head."

"Let's take a look at your head. There may be shrapnel hiding there, also."

Again, Dr. Rosenblum gently pressed and poked at a good-sized scar on the left side of Buzz's head. "Yes, there is something going on there. Let me do some reading and thinking about it. In the meantime, just say 'yes' or 'no' without head movement." He smiled and stood to go. "I will order something to help with the pain and see you Monday morning. Enjoy your family."

Buzz leaned back into his pillow and brought images of Midge and Bobby to mind. He closed his eyes. *I will be so happy to see you both again. How long before I really get to go home? I don't want to take this pain with me. Can Dr. Rosenblum really get rid of it? I wonder where he came from. He has an accent. Did he say he was Jewish? I'm sure he is happy not to be over there right now. I wonder how he found his way to America.*

The pills took effect. Buzz was sound asleep.

CHAPTER 12

FAMILY REUNION

Mom was so giddy I was surprised she remembered to tell the Fletchers not to pick us up for church today. Sarge was secure in the backyard; Don would check on him. My guess was that he would snare this opportunity to walk the dog by himself. Mom and I were off to see my Dad!

As it happened, several wounded airmen had flown home with Dad, so the Base arranged transport for families to visit. That would be us. Travel is difficult with tires and gas rationed, and we didn't even have a car.

Mom looked so pretty, her eyes sparkling with happiness. She kept fussing with me, although I was taller than she was then. I pointed to an oversize van stopped at the corner. "Don't you think we should go?"

Our 30-mile trip took almost an hour, due to the 35-mile speed restriction. This place was huge, but people guided us to Dad's room. We stood in the hall, savoring the moment, until Dad's voice called, "Will you two come in here? I can't hug you from my bed."

Mom rushed in, and they embraced, tears soaking her hair, her dress, and Dad's pillow and gown. I held back, happy to take it all in. Then Dad pretended to look behind Mom and under the bed for that boy he left behind. "Come here, son. Let me have a look at you."

I went to the other side of his bed. It was clear that Mom was not going to let go of his hand. I leaned in for his hug, afraid I'd hurt him if I hugged him like I wanted to. His left arm was bandaged, as was his head. Just seeing his injuries made a painful tingle run through my feet and fingers, and tears popped into my eyes. I looked away and grabbed a chair to sit close.

We wanted to know how he was doing, but all that interested Dad was home. He asked about the neighborhood, our friends, and my school. He couldn't seem to absorb enough of being home again. I told him about Sarge and pulled out a photo Don had taken for me.

At last, we got around to his injuries and what would happen. When he mentioned Dr. Rosenblum, Mom and I looked at each other. *Could it be the same Dr. Rosenblum who patched Sarge up?* So, then we had to bring Dad up to date on Sarge's incident.

"I can't imagine someone shooting a dog, especially one as nice-looking as Sarge." He tapped the photo. "Where do you think the dog went?"

"Well, Don and I walk him up to a big empty field to let him run," I said. "I think he might have found his way up there to chase rabbits."

"No one should be shooting that close to houses," Dad said. "Bullets just keep going, even the small-caliber ones." He gave me a knowing look just like he did when I was younger. "Do you know who might have done it?"

I didn't want to upset Dad, but I didn't want to lie, either. "I have a suspicion as to who it was. I'll find out."

"You be cautious, son. It's not good to get someone cornered, especially someone as reckless as this person seems to be." Then he turned back to Mom. "I'd like to walk a bit—sort of show off to my family."

I grabbed his robe and, with Dad in a wheelchair, we strolled down the hall. The place was orderly but busy. We even managed lunch with him until he began to look tired, and we returned to his room.

When it came time to leave, I could see that Mom wanted to stay, to be there with Dad to talk with the doctor. "Mom, stay here. It's okay. If it weren't for Sarge and school, I'd stay, too."

"Will you be okay, Bobby? Can you get yourself off to school? What about Sarge?"

"Mom," I said. "I'm almost sixteen. I'll do fine . . . so will Sarge. You need to be here with Dad. Be sure to call me tomorrow after you talk with the doctor." I could see her bottom lip trembling, so I thought fast. "Maybe Don can bring a sleeping bag and stay with me. I know his mom will feed me."

Dad chuckled. "Do you think his parents are up to feeding two of you?" He knocked his knuckles to mine, something we started doing when I was younger. "Thanks for leaving Mom here with me. It will be good to have her here when we meet with Dr. Rosenblum."

They waved me off. I think they were happy to have their own time together. I found the van and rode back home. Sarge was out of his mind to see me again.

"Good boy," I said. "Did you have fun with Don? We'll walk over to see if he can spend the night, but first I want to write about this day, so I never forget. I waited so long for it to come."

To Myself,

I do not want to forget this day . . . ever! It's February 27, 1944, and I saw my Dad again after almost two years. He's not home yet, but in the military hospital at Brigham City. He's where he needs to be, for now, to get his wounds taken care of. When his plane was hit, shrapnel wound up in his left shoulder and on the left side of his head. I almost cried when I saw him all bandaged up and weak. My heart, though, was thumping wildly with happiness. It was almost like being two people: one of me ready to collapse with relief, the other wanting to dance and sing. Neither of those are truly me, but that's how I felt.

Mom, too, was so happy she scarcely let go of his hand all the time I was there. I'm sure neither she nor Dad can get their fill of seeing each other again. It must have been so hard for her all this time. At least, I had school, Scouts, and my friends. Until she met the Fletchers and the McDowells, she had no one really. We sure couldn't count the crowd at that first church. I think she was afraid the whole time Mueller was living in that room in the attic and eating with us. What a trial that was! Dad doesn't know, but I'll tell him about it once he's home and getting better.

Dad met with, of all people, Dr. Rosenblum about surgery on that shoulder. He's been in a lot of pain with it, as well as his head. It must have been horrible in the POW camp, and then on that escape route. I'm looking forward to hearing about all that . . . when he's ready to talk about it. Mom will call me after school tomorrow, so I know what's up with the surgery. I hope Dr. Rosenblum can fix Dad up as well as he did Sarge. Funny world, isn't it—the way so many people are interconnected?

I never thought when I kicked that rock and hit Ruth's leg that she would be the one to find Sarge when he was shot . . . or that her dad might take the bullet out of Sarge, and now, the shrapnel out of Dad.

I heard a knock at the door. Sarge, learning to mind his manners, was having a hard time sitting while his tail was wound up like a propeller. Don was standing with his sleeping bag under one arm and some sort of supper in his hand.

He stepped inside. "Hi. Your mom called my mom, and here I am with supper and my bed. Are you ready for some company?"

"You bet. And thanks for seeing to Sarge while I was gone."

"He's no problem. Walking him gives me an excuse not to play another game of *Old Maid* with Sharon. I get tired of being the Old Maid to keep a six-year-old from pouting." Don rolled his eyes. "Let's eat, and you tell me about your dad."

Over venison meatloaf and macaroni with fake cheese, I filled Don in on my trip to the hospital. "It was so neat to see my Dad again. He's thin and all bandaged up—but happy to be this close to home. And, get this! Ruth's dad is who will be doing surgery on my Dad. I think it's going to take a while before he comes home. I'm just glad he's alive and here."

CHAPTER 13

SURGERY IS SCHEDULED

I could tell Mom's choices were eating at her. Was it okay to leave me on my own again so she could be with Dad during his X-rays and then surgery? What if I got sick, or hurt, or . . . ? All those things that moms fuss over. I had to call in Angie McDowell as backup to reassure Mom that she would keep an eye on me and Don.

"I'll be fine, Mom. Your job is to be with Dad. Mr. McDowell said he'd see I got on the van Saturday to join you." She wiped an eye and waved at me from the front door as I secured the gate. "Don't forget to put Sarge in the back yard. I'll see you Saturday. Hug Dad for me."

I joined Don to wade through the new snow and meet Laura Ann at her mailbox. She was stamping her boots to keep her legs warm and complaining again about wearing skirts when the guys get to wear jeans. I think she probably has a good argument. I wouldn't want to wear a skirt in this weather . . . or ever.

"So sad, too bad," Don teased. "Be grateful for those knee sox. I wish I had some."

She threw a mitten full of snow his way and then looked at me. "Why so quiet, Bobby? Sarge okay? Your Dad in more pain?"

"Maybe he won't be after this week. Mom stayed at the hospital to be there for X-rays and possible shoulder surgery."

"I'm sure he'll do much better once the doctor removes all that shrapnel," Don said.

"You know," I said. "I think he's really looking forward to surgery. I guess weeks of constant pain gets to a person. He was shot down in early January. That's a long time to be hurting. And, guess what? The doctor who removed Sarge's bullet will be taking the shrapnel out for Dad."

"No kidding! Maybe Dr. Rosenblum is your family's guardian angel." Don said. "Sarge was sure lucky Ruth found him."

"He sure was. Me, too. And I got an idea." I stopped us to get their attention. "Ruth must get lonely. She goes to school in Brigham City while her dad is at the hospital. That makes it hard for her to find friends here. What do you think about having one of our game nights and including her? Once Dad's on the mend, I'm sure Mom would help arrange it. Say, a Monday evening. That's when her dad comes back here to visit his patients on Tuesday."

"I'd love that," Laura Ann said. "Maybe start with something silly like *Battleship, Go Fish*, or . . . I can borrow Jackie's *Old Maid* cards."

"Hey, I've had enough of being the Old Maid with Sharon, but the rest sounds good," Don said.

The school bell rang.

▲　▲　▲

I really liked woodshop, but it's a double-edged sword these days with Arnie in class.

I was sure he was the one who shot Sarge. It was hard not to accuse him in front of everyone. I'd like to see his expression then. Would he laugh? Deny it? Get angry? I knew I needed to be patient. He was bound to let something slip. Then what would I do?

Mom's birdhouse began to take shape. Seemed Arnie was having a tough time getting the measurements right for his gun rack. Mr. Swanson spent most of the class period trying to get him straightened out.

"That's what I had writ down, Mr. Swanson," Arnie repeated.

"No, Arnie. You had 5 3/8. Try making your numbers legible."

"What's not legible? I can read my own numbers," Arnie insisted.

"Remember the rule," Mr. Swanson said. "Measure twice, cut once. You don't want that .22 falling off the rack."

Guys in class snickered. Arnie kicked a box. "What's so funny?"

Jay looked over at him. "How's your target practice going, Arnie?"

"Haven't had a chance to get out recently. But I did shoot a coyote a few weeks ago."

My ruler and pencil both fell to the floor.

"You did what?" Jay said as he stared Arnie in the face. "There aren't any coyotes in town."

"Yep, that's what it was. Hit it, too." Arnie took his bragging stance. "Tried to get another shot off, but it limped away. I'll get it next time."

Mr. Swanson stood in front of Arnie. "Just where are you doing your shooting?"

"There's some open fields up toward the mountains. It's okay. I know what I'm doing."

Mr. Swanson looked around the class. "Do any of you know that area? Do people go up there?"

"Yeah, I take my dog up there to throw sticks and his ball," I said. "He prefers chasing rabbits, though."

Mr. Swanson gave Arnie a warning look. "Doesn't sound like a place you should be shooting."

"I know the difference between Bobby and a coyote, Mr. Swanson. I'm not that stupid."

"Sometimes I wonder," Jay mumbled.

I was so angry, my hands were shaking. Big as Arnie was, I wanted to punch him in the face, knock him to the floor, and punch some more.

Jay noticed.

▲ ▲ ▲

Don and I were batchin' it again at my house. At least that's what we pretended.

Of course, his mom called when supper was ready. We took Sarge for a walk first. He pranced along between us as if to tell the world *Look, I have two boys all my own.* We did some homework and talked.

"Arnie admitted in class that he wounded what he called a coyote. I was so angry I was shaking. Mr. Swanson tried to talk some sense into him."

"Can't put smarts where there's only stupid," Don said. "Why is he such a goon?"

That question lay unanswered as the phone rang.

"Hi, Mom." I bombarded her with questions. "How's Dad? What about surgery? You'll call me after school, won't you? Can I come up on the van Saturday?"

Mom laughed as she fielded all my questions. Then she put Dad on.

"So good to talk to you, Dad. I'm sure Dr. Rosenblum will take good care of you. I'll be thinking of you all that day and waiting for Mom to call." I paused. "And, Dad, keep her there as long as you want. Don't worry about me. Don's good company, his mom feeds us, and I do have Sarge."

We bantered a bit, but long-distance calls were limited these days. I hung up the phone to find Don studying me. "So, what?" I asked him, spreading out my hands.

"Sometimes I wonder how you do like you do, Bob. Your life is so different from mine, or even Laura Ann's. Sure, we had to relocate due to the war, but our families stayed together." He shook his head. "I don't know how you and your mom managed with your dad overseas for so long—not to mention your unwelcome guest."

I had all but forgotten about Mueller, our Nazi spy. For security reasons, we were not supposed to talk about him. But the three of us did anyway.

"Do you sometimes wonder if all that really did happen, Don? It seems like a dream. But I guess we wouldn't all three have identical dreams. Wonder if he's still in prison, or what."

"Dad doesn't talk about his work, and I don't ask. Maybe, someday, when the war is over, he'll say." He got up to let Sarge out the back door. "I have to hand it to Laura Ann. She was one gutsy gal. Dad was impressed with her."

"I guess there's enough bad stuff going on here at home to keep your dad busy with his investigations." Sarge was scratching to get back in.

"I'm not supposed to hear things, but I think there is a lot of black-market stuff going on."

"Black market? I heard about it, but I'm not sure what it is."

Don looked around as if he thought someone might be eavesdropping. "You know how so much stuff is rationed and lots of things just plain unavailable? Well, it seems if you know the right people and have the money, you can get stuff. People cheat, steal, and hijack scarce items and sell them for big bucks. You know, gas, tires, meat, ration stamps. All that wheelin' and dealin' is the black market. Folks are even rustling cattle."

"Jeepers, Don," I said. "That was fifty years ago. Only movie stars like Roy Rogers and Gene Autry chase rustlers these days."

"Nope, it's true. With beef rationed and scarce to boot, a steak is worth big money. Dad said Americans just got used to having what they wanted and don't like going without, so there's a ready market—even if it's black. 'Course, most people pitch in for the war effort, but there are those who break the law. He's tracking gasoline cheaters in the area now. But you and I don't know that." He winked and got up to answer the door.

"Mom sent me to come get you and Bobby, Donnie." It was his little sister Sharon. "And," in a bossy tone, she added, "don't be late!" She giggled when he tossed some snow after her.

I checked on Sarge in the backyard before we crossed the street to Don's house.

CHAPTER 14

X-rays Tell the Tale

The days could not pass fast enough. I felt like I did when Sarge was missing and all I wanted to do was skip school and go search for him. Today Mom would call with news about Dad's X-rays and operations, so I hustled home. I spent a few minutes brushing Sarge and refilling his water pan. The phone rang.

"Hi, Mom," I said.

Laughter answered me. "Hi, Bobby. It's Dad. Your Mom is in the van heading home. I was so glad to have her here with me. Did you manage okay?"

"Golly, Dad," I said. "It's great to hear *you* on the phone. I'm fine. I was just thinking about you."

"Well, your Mom and I met with Dr. Rosenblum this morning. He had taken X-rays of my arm and shoulder, and he let us see them. It was amazing, but even I could see why I've had so much pain." I heard the excitement in his voice. "He pointed out several pieces of shrapnel lodged in my shoulder, even though the wounds had healed over. Dr. Rosenblum said that is what helped keep infection out. I have that POW medic to thank for that. Dr. Rosenblum will operate on the shoulder Thursday to remove that shrapnel and clean up the wound."

"Are you worried, Dad?" I was worried just thinking about him having to have his arm cut open again.

"Not if you'll let your Mom come back up to be with me." I could hear the teasing in his voice . . . just like before he left for the war.

"Yeah, sure, Dad. I'm fine . . . and I have to stay here to take care of Sarge."

"Thanks, Bobby. We'll see about getting you up here again on the weekend."

"Uh, Dad. What about your head injury? Does it still hurt like it did?"

There was some silence on the line. "Let's take this one step at a time, okay?" Dad said. "I'd better go now. Can't tie up the phone. Mom will fill you in. Love you, son."

I sat and thought about my Dad. I knew he was tough, especially after all he had gone through since his plane went down. He doesn't seem worried about his shoulder surgery—he even acted as if he were looking forward to it. I think he has confidence in Dr. Rosenblum." I placed the phone back in its cradle. *The head injury is the real problem,* I thought to myself. *I don't believe he's told everything about that . . . or, not to me. I'll ask Mom what she knows tonight.*

"Hey, Sarge." I grabbed his leash. "Shall we go exercise that gimpy leg of yours?" He still favored it a bit, but I was sure exercise couldn't hurt. "You have to stay on the leash for a while longer. No rabbits or squirrels." His tail was wagging his whole back end, so I took that as a *Yes.*

The wind was cold, so I tugged on my aviator cap. It was getting a bit tight. *Maybe Dad can get me a new one.* I clipped the leash on Sarge and pulled on my gloves. "Hey, boy, why don't we walk up by Ruth's house to see if she's home? We really need to thank her dad for patching you up."

Sarge trotted along beside me, delighted to be out. My walk was brisk against the wind coming off the mountains. We stopped in front of Ruth's house. *Was she home? Only one way to find out.* As I opened the gate, a voice called from the open door.

"Hi, Bobby! How's my favorite dog doing?" Ruth motioned us in. "Come in out of that wind. Dad's home. He'll be glad to see his furry patient."

I knelt on the carpet beside Sarge and looked around. I'd never been in a doctor's home before, but I was sure this is what it should look like. Books, and more books, a briefcase and black medical bag, bifocals on every surface.

Ruth led her father into the room. "Papa, this is Bobby Bradley. Sarge is his dog."

"Hello, Bobby. I think we met at the hospital, yes?" He got down on the floor next to Sarge. "And, how are you doing, fellow?" He let Sarge sniff his hands, and then he rubbed his ears and talked to him. He looked over at me. "We have to get reacquainted, you know." He moved his hands along Sarge's flank to where his wound was. Sarge turned his head to watch what he was doing but stayed calm.

Dr. Rosenblum stood and motioned me to take a seat. "He is doing fine. I'm glad you are giving him a bit of exercise to stretch that leg. That was a nasty thing to happen to him. I'm glad Ruth saw him and that I was home to help."

"Thank you so much, Dr. Rosenblum, for treating him. Is there any way I can repay you? I had lots of folks helping me search for him." I hugged Sarge. "I was afraid for him, like I was for my Dad when his plane went down." I had to swallow to calm myself. "It's terrible not knowing."

"Yes, we know how that is." Dr. Rosenblum sat down next to Ruth. "Don't we, Ruth?"

She moved closer to her dad. *Was there something in their lives that wasn't good? Where was Ruth's mother? Had something bad happened to her?*

Dr. Rosenblum continued. "You are wondering where Ruth's mother is, and I will explain. We are from Austria, where I was a surgeon and taught at the University. Our family was happy there. When the Nazis took over, Ruth and I had to leave. They are not so good to Jewish people. Her mother is German, or, as the Nazis say, *Aryan*, so she was safe. She did go to England with us, and we were there for some time. However, the Nazis took over the family home, and food for Austrians became scarce. Her parents are elderly, and her brothers are all in the German military, so Hildy insisted on returning to care for them. We pray this war will be over soon so she can join us here."

My fist clenched Sarge's leash as I listened to their story. "I am so sorry. You must miss her very much." I looked at Ruth. "I know how much I missed Dad for almost two years. I really didn't expect to see him again until the war's end." I looked from one to the other. "There must be some way I can help you."

"You are doing it, Bobby," the doctor said. "Ruth left her friends behind, so it is good you came to visit. I am at the hospital four days a week, and I take Ruth with me. She gets lessons but it is not like being with other young people. Today I am in town here to visit patients who have returned home. After some weeks, your Dad may be on that list."

I stood to go. "My Mom will be home soon, so I better get going. Thanks again from me and Sarge. Is Monday the day you are home every week? I have friends I know would love to meet Ruth."

"That would be nice for Ruth. Thank you, and take care of Sarge," the doctor said.

"Thank you for tending my Dad *and* my dog." I smiled. "See you later."

▲ ▲ ▲

I stepped outside to find the wind gone and feathery snow falling. I moseyed home, letting Sarge sniff and leave a trail of yellow snow. The van had just dropped Mom off as we reached the gate.

Mom looped her arm through mine. "I have lots to tell you, Bobby." We hung our coats and she looked around. "You seem to have managed okay. Shall we have breakfast for supper tonight? Maybe even pancakes?"

"Anything is fine with me, Mom. I want to know about Dad."

Over supper, she filled me in on Dad's X-rays and his surgery. It seemed the only way to get rid of the pain in his arm and shoulder was to remove the shrapnel. She avoided talking about the head wound. *Yeah, I know, one step at a time.*

Mom took up some mending and was humming along to Glenn Miller's band on the radio. I was glad to see Mom so relaxed. I wish I were. There were too many different thoughts crowding around in my mind. I was happy Dad was home, but his head injury still concerned me. I was scared that surgery might not go so well, seeing as how it was so close to his brain.

I had been so thankful I got Sarge back and that Dr. Rosenblum took care of that bullet wound. Yet I always wondered if it was Arnie who shot him—and what I could do about that. Meeting Ruth was a plus, but I felt badly that her mom was back in in Austria. Perhaps Laura Ann, Don and I could help Ruth settle in and not be so lonely. Dr. Rosenblum thought that was a good idea.

I bopped myself on the side of the head to make sense of all my thoughts. They seemed to be swirling around. I couldn't make heads or tails of anything. I pulled out a sheet of paper. Maybe Dad could come up with ideas.

Hi Dad,

> *Mom got home okay from the hospital today. In spite of your upcoming arm surgery, she seems relaxed and happy. Mostly to just have you home again. I'm happy too, of course, but I want to talk with you about just stuff, and now doesn't seem the right time.*
>
> *I'm going to ask to see your X-rays—of the arm and the head. I don't think I would worry so much if you and Mom didn't think I needed to be protected. My imagination runs wild with all the "what ifs." I mostly worry about the head surgery. What if the shrapnel is really deep? Will you have any brain damage, and what kind? How long will you stay in the hospital?*
>
> *And then, what about Sarge getting shot? I do believe I know who shot him, but what can I do about it, if anything? I plan to investigate, but I won't do anything stupid. I'm glad you reminded me that it could be dangerous to confront Arnie. He is a bully and a hothead, but he's afraid of his dad. I guess I should be, too.*
>
> *Most important is for you to get through this first surgery. And, the second one, too. My problems can wait.*

Love you, Bobby.

CHAPTER 15

Arnie's Afraid

Friday, I used tack cloth to wipe the birdhouse clean from sanding and left it on the side table. It was ready for its first coat of paint on Monday. I hurried home to take Sarge for a long walk. While I am with Mom and Dad at the hospital over the weekend, Don will tend Sarge.

Mom called to say the surgery on Dad's arm had gone well. I looked forward to seeing him and hearing all about it—and what's happening next. Getting information out of my parents was a challenge these days. Did they still see me as some tender kid they had to shield from the truth? I know Dad's head hurts, probably all the time, though he tries to brush it aside. I can see the pain behind his eyes when he jokes, and how he winces when he moves his head. Operating on someone's skull is serious. One slip of the knife . . . and I don't want to think about it.

When I opened the front gate, I could hear Sarge jumping at the back door and raising the kind of fuss dogs are good at. He greeted me with slobbery kisses and that whipping tail. I clicked on his leash, and we set out up the hill. Don was babysitting little Sharon, so it was just me and Sarge. We walked up to where the sidewalk ended in deep drifts. Sarge made yellow snow; then he danced around until I undid his leash and pulled his red ball from my pocket. He was like a ballplayer backing into left field as he waited for my pitch. Off he went.

I heard a rifle shot. My heart skipped six or seven beats. I couldn't breathe. Did someone shoot at Sarge? I whistled and about fainted in relief when Sarge bounded back with his ball. He dropped it in the snow and then lay at my feet, whining and trembling. Was he hit? I felt him all over. He was unhurt but frightened. I guess he'd recognized that loud *pop* from when he was shot.

"It's okay, boy. Scared me, too. Let's find out who's shooting, but I think I know."

I pulled off my red scarf and wrapped it around my head as I searched for the shooter. There was Arnie, in the distance, aiming into some treetops. I yelled at him and started his way. With each step, I grew angrier.

Arnie stood his ground, holding the .22 and glaring at me.

"Point that thing to the ground, you idiot," I yelled.

"Just what are you going to do if I don't?" He hadn't lowered the rifle, but it wasn't pointed right at me. "And don't call me an idiot!"

It seemed to be a standoff, until Sarge stepped in front of me. His hackles were standing on end, and his lips curled back to show bared fangs. A growl rumbled deep in his throat. I was as surprised as Arnie. Except Arnie was scared.

"Don't you s-s-sic that dog on me. That dog looks like a really m-m-mean one." Arnie had lowered the .22 and backed away. His face lost color, and his hands were shaking. "If that dog bites me, my dad will come after you." He turned and stumbled through the snow, glancing over his shoulder to make sure Sarge was not in pursuit.

I just stood there with my hand resting on Sarge's head. "Can you beat that, Sarge? The big bully is afraid of dogs." I clipped on his leash. "Of course, the way you looked, *I'd* be afraid of you, too." I ruffled his ears. "I think a Chihuahua would frighten him. Come on, I'll throw the ball a bit more."

As we headed home, I thought about Arnie. Was he mostly bluster? He was sneaky and underhanded, like when he knocked my plane to the floor and his foot just happened to crush the wing. Then he was full of gleeful swagger and just sauntered off. This encounter was different, and I felt I'd discovered some useful bits of information: He doesn't like being called out, and he is deathly afraid of dogs. I planned to learn more about my Arnie boy.

▲ ▲ ▲

I'd just finished giving Sarge food and fresh water when Don came to the door with bowls of chili and a bag of apple-sauce cookies. *Applesauce cookies seem to be the mainstay for moms these days. With sugar rationed, apples supply the sweetener.* We sat on the carpet, leaning against furniture, to catch up on the day. I related my meeting with Arnie.

"Weren't you just a bit uneasy yelling at him like that? He was the one with the rifle, you know."

"Maybe I should have been, but I was the one with the dog, Don. And Arnie is afraid of dogs. I've been thinking a lot about him. He plays like the big, tough bully and gets away with it because of his size. Is he really that good in football?"

"He mostly depends on his size to just roll over the other guys. That's why he likes offense, as opposed to defense. I'm not sure he likes mixing it up." Don chomped a third cookie and changed the subject. "So, got any instructions for tomorrow? I know where Sarge's food is. And, his ball and brush. If my mom wasn't allergic to animal fur, I'd take him home. But, we'll do fine here. I'll walk him both days you're gone." Sarge was now stretched out between us, lapping up cookie crumbs. "You know, Bob, I really appreciate you sharing him with me."

I patted Sarge's side. "He likes it, too. He believes he's the only shepherd who owns two boys."

CHAPTER 16

More Issues

Saturday morning, I climbed into the van, eager to see Dad but with mixed emotions about leaving Sarge. I knew he would be okay with Don, but I'd miss him. Before long I was walking into the hospital to find Mom waiting for me and looking so happy.

"Bobby, your Dad came through his surgery with flying colors." She grabbed my hand as she's done as long as I can remember. "Did you get along okay?" She squeezed my fingers.

"I did fine, Mom," I said. "I'm old enough to stay on my own, and I do have Sarge."

She grinned up at me. "I know, I know. But I am the mom, and I will worry if I want to."

I was taller than her, and, in my eagerness to see Dad, I walked a bit too fast for her. "Slow down, Bobby. I can't keep up with you anymore. Oh, here's room 105. He's in this recovery room now."

We more or less tiptoed into his room, in case he might be sleeping. Nothing wrong with Dad's hearing. "Hey, you two, come on in. I want to see how much Bobby's grown in the past couple weeks."

I found Dad sitting up in a chair, his arm heavily bandaged . . . and his head, too. I pointed, "What's all this?"

"Bad headaches, so Dr. Rosenblum did a bit of probing. Once my arm is healing well, he plans on removing the shrapnel there." Dad grinned at me, but I noticed something else behind his eyes. *I knew I wasn't getting the full story here.*

Mom, of course, changed the subject. "How about we go to the cafeteria for a bite? I bet Bobby's hungry."

Because of his head injury, Dad had to go in a wheelchair. I pushed as Mom walked alongside, grasping his hand as if he might up and disappear. Little was said about hospital stuff. They wanted to know about school and Sarge.

"School is fine, and Don and I enjoy just hanging out evenings. His mom is good to provide enough rations. Don likes walking Sarge with me. He'd love to have a dog of his own."

Dad gave me a steady look. "And this kid you suspect shot him—any more ideas in that department?"

I hadn't planned on talking about my encounter with Arnie and his rifle. Mom would get all fussed over it, but Dad might have some suggestions. So, I told them what happened.

Mom did her fussing, but Dad was thoughtful. "So, this bully is not such a bully when threatened by Sarge? Any ideas why?"

"Nope. Arnie turned tail with his .22 and left the field. Not without threatening me with his own dad if Sarge bit him." I reached down to pat my dog's head, forgetting he was home with Don. "I'm going to find out more about Arnie and his dad. I've learned where he lives."

Mom had her hand over her mouth, but Dad was direct. "I know you think you need to follow up on this, but be careful. This kid and his attitude about firearms is unhealthy, to say the least. It's good you have Sarge with you."

"I'll use my head, Dad. Don't worry about me. I'm so glad to have the weekend to spend with you."

It was nice to be a family again, but the time passed quickly. Mom rode the van home with me, planning to go back to the hospital Thursday, when Dad would see Dr. Rosenblum again. On the way home, I sounded her out about arranging a game night and inviting Ruth to join us. We chose a Monday.

▲　▲　▲

On the way to school, I set up game night with Don and Laura Ann. It would be fun to get together again. I toughed the day out through English and science, glad to finally go downstairs to shop class. I'd planned to prime the birdhouse today and paint it tomorrow.

When I walked into class, I saw Arnie at the back of the room, again wearing his smug look. I picked up the birdhouse to take to my bench and almost attacked Arnie right then. There were deep pencil gouges in the once-smooth roof. I could feel my face flush as I banged my fist on the bench.

Mr. Swanson came over. "What's wrong, Bobby? You were going to start priming today."

"Look at this, Mr. Swanson. Some imbecile," I glared back at Arnie. ". . . ruined that plan!"

One quick look, and the teacher walked to the back of the room. "What would you know about this, Arnie? I saw you at the project shelf."

No denial. "Sorry, Mr. Swanson, I think my pencil slipped a bit." Arnie glanced around the class for approval—and possible laughs. Only disgusted frowns met his look. He shrugged. "Well, Bobby's so clever he'll fix it in no time . . . like his plane."

"Jay," Mr. Swanson said. His voice bristled with anger. "Will you accompany Arnie to the principal's office and explain why he is to spend the rest of the school day sitting in central hall?" He turned to the culprit. "And, *you*—get out of here."

Arnie, head down, followed Jay out, but not without sending one hateful look my way. I felt some satisfaction, as all students knew anyone sitting in *that* hall was being punished.

I spent the class period sanding out the pencil gouges so that I could paint tomorrow. Mr. Swanson hovered nearby, checking to see how it was going.

I caught up with Jay after class. "Hey, any idea why I seem to be Arnie's target these days, Jay? I hardly knew him before this class."

"You've probably noticed that he's not the smartest chip off the block. He wants attention, even if it's bad." Jay brushed his over-long bangs out of his eyes. "I think there are a lot of family issues in that house. I hear the dad yelling at Arnie in the evenings. He's a truck driver and expects Arnie to jump when he says so."

"So, you live pretty close to him, right?"

"They live on the next street down, but there's an empty lot between us, so I can see their driveway from my house. I think the mom works at one of the plants. Word is that when his dad's draft number was about to come up, he got a job hauling freight to get a deferment. He was really afraid he would get called up." He flipped his hair again. "Not the most popular family in the neighborhood."

I decided against telling Jay about meeting up with Arnie and the rifle. *When Mom goes back up to Brigham City, maybe Don and I will walk Sarge that way. Might catch a glimpse of this all-American, patriotic dad of his.*

I waved Jay off and hurried home, so I had time to walk Sarge up to Ruth's to invite her for our game night. She was delighted.

CHAPTER 17

Game Night

Game Night was on. I walked Sarge to pick up Ruth at her home. Mom said it would be more comfortable for her than walking down by herself.

When Ruth answered the door, Sarge stepped right up as if he were her escort. She knelt and ruffled his ears. "How's my favorite dog today?" She smiled up at me, "Hi, Bobby. Let me tell my dad I'm leaving."

Dr. Rosenblum appeared. "Good to see you again, Bobby . . . and Sarge." My dog's backend rumbaed sideways at the sound of his name.

"Hi, Dr. Rosenblum. Thanks for repairing my dad's arm and putting smiles on both my parents' faces. I got to spend the weekend at the hospital. It was great." I held the door so that Ruth could step out. "Oh, my mom has made supper for all of us. I'll see that Ruth gets home safely, about 9:00, if that's okay."

He gave his daughter a quick hug. "You have a good time, *Liebchen*. I'll leave the porch light on for you."

▲　▲　▲

Laura Ann and Don were on the carpet, sorting out games when Ruth and I arrived. After some break-the-ice chatter, we decided to start with *Sorry*. Ruth caught on quickly and laughed when she could pull out a Sorry card.

"I had *keine Brueder oder Schwestern* to play with me in Austria. I mean *brothers or sisters*." She shook her head as she looked at all of us. "You must remember me to use English." She giggled and tapped her brain. "I mean *remind* me. My mother and father taught me chess, but games are more fun with friends."

"You and Laura Ann need to help each other," Don said. "She's been trying to learn German from her grandfather . . . through the mail. You two would be a great team."

Ruth perked up. "You are learning *Deutsch*?"

"Yes," Laura Ann said. "Grandpa started teaching me before we moved here. He sent me a German book to help, and my mom does the best she can with pronunciation. I do get lost." She rolled her eyes. "I could use your help."

"I think we can help each other," Ruth said. "I know that sometimes I use the wrong word, and I slip back into speaking German too often."

"Super," Laura Ann said. "We'll set up our own time . . . without guys." She grinned at Don and me.

That was fine with me. Ruth did need to be friends with another girl, and Laura Ann would help her find confidence. However, being best friends with two guys never bothered that girl. Laura Ann had been bullied by some local girls at the start, but soon, she started to stand her ground. It was as if she became *Wonder Woman*—or, more likely, *Nancy Drew*—almost overnight. We had quite an adventure last year. No doubt, she would help Ruth through the rough patches, but not too much. I liked Ruth the way she was.

My mom slipped into the room. "Are you four hungry yet? We're having spaghetti with toasted bread. I used canned peaches and made a cobbler."

We left the game board on the carpet. Ruth stood and looked at the three of us. "How do you say? No fair peeking at my hidden cards . . . or be Sorry." She giggled at her own joke.

The spaghetti was great. Mom put every fresh vegetable she could find into the sauce, with a bit of hamburger. With rationing and shortages, all moms got creative.

After eating our fill, we got back to the game. Ruth kept one eye on the clock. "I think it's time for me to go home. Papa will be watching for me. Thank you for inviting me. I have . . . er . . . had so much fun."

"School night for all of us," Don said as he grabbed his coat. "Bob and I will walk you girls to the corner and watch as Laura Ann heads home, and then walk you to your house, Ruth."

They all thanked Mom for the meal. It was dark outside, with a strong wind blowing again. Laura Ann trotted down the hill, and the three of us walked backwards into the wind to reach Ruth's street. On her porch, she thanked us both and disappeared inside.

Don and I headed back home. "When is your mom going back to the hospital, Bob?"

"Thursday, when they see Dr. Rosenblum. She may or may not stay through the weekend. Guess it depends on when Dad's head surgery is scheduled."

I was quiet for a few minutes. "You know, Don, I'm worried about this next surgery. I don't think I'm getting the full story on it. I'll be glad when Dad can be home to recover. Then we'll be a family again."

"That must be really hard. If you want my company, I'll check with my folks about staying with you."

"I'd like that."

CHAPTER 18

Reconnaissance

As it turned out, Mom stayed on at the hospital to be there for tests Dad would undergo, and Don would keep me company while she was gone. Or, at least, most of the time. Saturday afternoon, Sarge and I were on our own. This, I thought, was a good time to walk Sarge and check out how things were in Arnie's neighborhood.

I found Jay's house, and, sure enough, the lot across the street was empty, offering a perfect view of Arnie's backyard and driveway. I heard yelling coming from his house. "Arnie, how many times do I have to tell you to leave your sister alone? You wait until your dad gets home."

This might prove interesting, I thought. "Let's go toss the ball a bit and check back later, okay, Sarge?" We walked on a few blocks further until I could throw his ball for him. It was chilly but not windy. I'd bundled up for my reconnaissance trip.

It was late afternoon when I returned to Jay's neighborhood. I'd no sooner found a tree stump for my observation post when I heard an engine. A black truck and large tanker trailer was backing into Arnie's driveway. A much larger version of Arnie climbed down from the truck, slammed his door, and yelled for Arnie.

Arnie, tugging on his coat, appeared in the driveway. "Yeah, Dad, I'm here."

"Well, you know what to do. Get with it."

"It's not dark yet, Dad." A long pause. "Do I have to? It tastes terrible and I burp all night."

"You're not supposed to drink it, stupid. Give a quick suck and stick the hose in the gas can."

"But, dad. I think Donna needs to take a turn at this."

"What! She's a girl, probably doing her homework inside. This is your job." I ducked down as the man, hand raised, stalked over to his son. "No more whining. Remember last time you bellyached?"

Arnie shuffled to the garage and hauled a large can and length of hose to the tanker. He unscrewed the gas cap and inserted an end of the hose. He looked up to the darkening sky. I could make out an expression of revulsion on his face. Then he bent over the other end of the hose and put it in his mouth. Gagging and coughing, he quickly stuck that end into the gas can. I could hear gasoline hitting the bottom of the metal can.

What on earth was going on?

Wiping his mouth and spitting, Arnie lugged the heavy can and hose back to the garage.

His dad watched, laughing. "Someday you'll learn how to do it right, Arnie. Just don't try smoking until then."

The back door banged as Arnie stomped inside. A minute later there was a loud wail. "Arnie, quit taking everything out on your sister. Your dad will hear of this."

All this time a low growl was coming from Sarge's throat. I patted his flank. "Come on, boy. Time for us to get out of here."

We backed through the brush and started home. What a way to live! I'm glad I'm not in that family. I mulled over what I had seen, trying to make sense of it. The dad's been out on the road, making deliveries; then he comes home and makes Arnie suck gasoline out of the tanker and into a can. The extra gas is stored in the garage. Why?

▲　▲　▲

I was just finishing my second bowl of cereal for supper when Don tapped on the door. I set the bowl on the floor so that Sarge could lap up the last of the milk; then I went to let Don in.

Don tossed a bag of vegetables into the sink. "My folks thought your mom might be glad for some fresh stuff. Canned goods can be hard to come by. These friends we visited have an active root cellar. Not like yours, given over to spiders and spies." He laughed at his own cleverness.

"No spiders in that bag, are there?" I punched his arm.

We flopped on the living room sofa. He talked about his day, and then, he stopped and looked at me. "You've been up to something, Bob. Clue me in."

So, I did. Don listened intently. "I don't get it, Don. Why would his dad make Arnie suck gas out of his tanker to put in a can?"

"Oh, wow!" Don sat upright. "That's it! His dad's reselling the gas on the Black Market, I bet. And, that sucking is called *siphoning* the gas. I imagine having to do that really is pretty nasty. This might be what's going on. His dad does his hauling but siphons off any leftover gasoline and saves it. He can sell it on the Black Market. What I wonder is if he is then hitting the ration board up for more gas stamps . . . because his tank gets low. Have to keep supplies moving, you know." He shook his head. "All for the war effort, 'cause he's so patriotic. He could even be selling the extra gas stamps."

I thought this over for a few minutes. "Yep, he is siphoning gas all right. But isn't that illegal? It has to be."

"I'm sure it is," Don said. "Maybe I can get my dad into a discussion of the Black Market and cheating on stamps, and such. He will know what illegal activities are going on and maybe who's in charge of that. It won't be dad. He's more involved with military stuff."

"You know, for a second or two, I actually felt sorry for Arnie, watching him gag on the gas. Sarge didn't, though. He growled the whole time I watched."

▲ ▲ ▲

Mom got home Sunday evening. I pried as much information about Dad's head surgery out of her as I could. I knew she was worried, and that made me worried. It really upset me when she said I should stay home and go to school.

"Mom," I insisted. "I want to be with you during the surgery Thursday. I won't be able to concentrate on anything at school. I might as well help you wait and worry. I want to be there when he wakes up."

She sat down at the table and motioned to my chair. "Bobby, Dr. Rosenblum is not sure how an operation on Dad's head will go. There can be any number of side effects."

"But, what about that shrapnel he still has in his skull?" I was getting heated and argumentative—something I rarely do. "The headaches, the dizziness when he moves his head, his slurred speech. Aren't those side effects of his wound?" She looked stunned. "Oh, yeah, Mom, I've noticed those. I'm really not a little kid anymore."

Her eyes filled with tears. "No, you aren't, Bobby. And I would love to have you with me. We'll take the van together Wednesday to be with Dad. There are places for family to stay during procedures." She squeezed my hand. "You need to be there to ask Dr. Rosenblum your questions, too."

CHAPTER 19

WAITING FOR RESULTS

It seems about all Mom and I have done for the past two years is wait and worry. We ought to be experts at it by now. But we aren't. Mom wrings her hands and studies the clock, and then her wristwatch. Me? I wriggle in my chair, pace the floor, and pop my knuckles. Hours passed like weeks before Dr. Rosenblum appeared. He was not smiling.

He pulled a chair up close to us, leaned forward, fingers laced, and spoke softly.

"This was a tough surgery—there was so much scar tissue to cut away." He nodded and smiled a bit. "But I found and excised all three pieces of shrapnel." He shook a small bottle and handed it to me. "One was quite deep. We must pray that any damage it did will heal over time. I will watch for infection and brain swelling. The job for you two is to show patience and encouragement."

Mom cried softly into her handkerchief. He reached over and patted her hand. "Every head injury is serious, and recovery can be unpredictable. The medical community is still learning about the brain and how miraculous it is. Before the war, I studied the different areas of it with brilliant colleagues of mine. We did not all agree but learned from one another. Unfortunately, most of them had to flee Austria for England when I did." He sat upright. "Buzz is a strong man, a fighter all the way. He may get confused and even angry when he encounters difficulty with simple tasks, or with speech. That is to be expected . . . but he may not think so. The surgery itself was successful, and he will heal. Recovery may offer some hurdles. I am not sure just what, but I will help you help him."

Dr. Rosenblum stood. "It may be several hours before Captain Bradley awakens. I'll have a nurse find you when he rouses so that you can tell him 'goodnight.' For now, you two take a walk, get a bite to eat. Time is what you all need now. No more worries. I will meet with you tomorrow." He patted my shoulder. "I will try to find Ruth and send her to beat you at a game of checkers."

With a quick goodbye, he left. Mom and I looked at each other. Tears were running down her cheeks, and I felt my eyes fill with tears. At the same moment, we let out a breath of relief and laughed. "I had no idea I was holding my breath so long," Mom said.

"Do you suppose he left so we could breathe again?" I put my arms around Mom and hugged her. "You know, Mom, I do believe you are getting smaller."

"Come—let's get some fresh air."

▲　▲　▲

We had just finished eating when a nurse showed up. "Mrs. Bradley? Your husband is coming around if you two would like to see him. He is confused, but I know he'll be glad to see you. Just don't expect too much right now."

She led us to Dad's recovery room. Tears choked me when I saw both his head and arm swaddled in bandages. His right hand reached up for Mom as he gave a weak smile.

"Don't try to talk, Buzz," Mom said. "Bobby and I just needed to check on you. You rest and get strong."

Dad motioned for us to sit down and to move our chairs close to his bed. The nurse brought a glass of water with a straw. He indicated that Mom should take over and the nurse should leave. "It seems Captain Bradley is still giving orders." She winked and left.

Mom held his hand and assured him the surgery had gone well. I held up the shrapnel pieces for him to see. He nodded his head and smiled, letting us know the sharp pain was gone. Then he dozed off. We sat with him for a while without words. It was enough just to be a family again.

The nurse returned. "It seems Captain Bradley has landed his plane for the night. He needs to rest." She picked up his wrist to check his pulse. "I'll keep watch tonight. You both look exhausted. You are okay for beds for the night, aren't you?"

Reluctantly, Mom tucked Dad's hand under his blanket and found a spot without bandages to place a quick kiss. Out in the hall, I found Ruth waiting for us.

"Hi," she said softly. "Dad said the surgery went well. I'm happy for that. Are you up for a game of checkers, Bobby? I must warn you—I'm pretty good."

I looked at Mom. "You go ahead, Bobby. I'll grab a few magazines and go to our room. I need to unwind a bit."

Ruth led me to a recreation room, pulled out a checker game, and set it up on a table. We played several games and wound up tied. "You hold your own at checkers," she said.

"Yeah, sometimes. Don and I play, but he prefers chess. All I do is move the pieces in the wrong direction." I gave a hopeless shrug. "You need to challenge him someday. I'd like to watch that match."

We pushed the checkers aside. "I'm looking forward to getting my Dad home again," I said. "It's been so long since we have been a family."

Ruth's face clouded. "*Ich auch.* Uh . . . I mean it's the same for me. I really miss my mom. Dad does his best for me, but I know he misses her, too. It's been two years since I last saw her. I was ten when we escaped to England. You see, my dad has a Jewish heritage, and mom is what the Nazis call "Aryan".

Long ago, dad made the decision to attend church with mom. Everything was fine until the Nazis took over and started persecution of the Jewish people. It didn't matter that he was a Christian Jew—he was still a Jew to them. It was unsafe for dad to stay in Austria. Me, too, as I am half-Jewish. So, the three of us left for England."

She sent me an apologetic smile. "Are you sure you want to hear all this, Bobby?"

"Well, sure, Ruth. I had no idea how things really were, or are, in Europe."

"Oh, it is very bad over there now. The Nazis have total power. Some German people believe and support them, but others are truly frightened. We got out in time and were safe, but mom worried about her parents back in Vienna. Her three older brothers were away in the military, so my mom felt responsible for my grandparents." She paused. "It's all so wrong, Bobby."

"I can't argue there, Ruth. This war doesn't care whose lives it messes with. Don's and Laura Ann's families had to move, but they stayed together. For you and me, it's different." I still didn't understand why her mother wasn't with her. So, I asked.

"Your mom went to England with you and your dad but then went back to Austria? How did that happen?"

Ruth sighed. "My mom could still receive letters from her parents when we were in England, but the news was not good. The Nazi command took over my grandparents' lovely home and moved them into a caretaker's cottage on the property. When they found my grandfather's radio, they threatened to send them to a work camp. My grandmother was so afraid; she cried at night and was afraid to go out to market. My grandfather is loyal to Austria, but not to the Nazis. He is also quite stubborn and does not know when to keep quiet."

"Yeah, I have a grandpa like that down in Texas. The Nazis would have their hands full with him, too, I'm afraid."

Ruth twisted her wet handkerchief into a knot. "When Mutti learned that he had been beaten . . . that's when she returned to Austria. She thought she could keep them safe. It's been almost two years now, and life is very hard there. Food goes to the soldiers, not to the people. We receive few letters, mostly through the Red Cross or Jewish underground." That handkerchief now mopped her eyes. "I am afraid for her, Bobby, and my grandparents. I wish she was here and safe with us."

Her bottom lip trembled, and she looked away. "Sometimes, Bobby, I can't think what she looks like. I have to go find a photograph. I feel like I have lost her." She brushed tears away. "I don't know if she is okay. Does she have food enough to eat? Are my grandparents okay, or even alive?"

I reached my hand across the table. "I'm so sorry, Ruth. Until my Dad was shot down, I missed him, but I always felt he was safe. He was supposed to be training pilots, not flying into combat himself."

"How did he get shot down then, Bobby?"

"He and his wingman, that's his flying partner, were regulating some instrument flying, I think. The *Luftwaffe* planes flew out of the clouds, and the battle was on. His plane went down." I felt shivers remembering the day we got the news he was missing. "It was awful. Was he alive, dead? Was he hurt? Captured? We had no word, except that he was missing in action. I had to get out his photo, too."

"It's terrible, isn't it, Bobby? I try to remember my Mutti's voice, and how she used to sing. We would sing together, and then dad would join in."

I saw a smile on Ruth's face.

CHAPTER 20

COMPLICATIONS

I crept into the guest room that Mom and I shared. She was sound asleep, exhausted from worry over Dad and these surgeries. Once in bed, I lay there with my own thoughts knocking around in my head—Dad, Sarge, Arnie, and now Ruth. I couldn't remember when life was peaceful and each day was pleasant. War stirs everyone into its stewpot.

Seems I'd just dozed off when I heard the door latch, and Mom, framed by the hall light, slipped in. I clicked on the bedside lamp. "Mom, is everything all right? Dad?"

She sat on the edge of her bed, her hands wrapped around her coffee cup. "Sorry to disturb you, Bobby. I woke, couldn't get back to sleep, and, so, I went to sit with your Dad. He was calm then, but the nurse said he had been restless and mumbled in his sleep. Dr. Rosenblum won't be in for another hour or so." She sipped her coffee and smiled at me. "I am really glad you're here with me. When I'm alone, the waiting is hard."

I flipped my feet over the edge of my bed and sat up. "You and I are veterans at waiting, Mom. But it's always hard. Once we get Dad home, we can be a family, like we used to be."

Her face clouded. "Let's pray his recovery goes well, that there are no . . . complications." She laced fingers around her cup, a sure sign she was afraid.

"Then we need to talk about these *complications*, don't ya think?" I slipped into the bathroom and dressed. "Let's go get breakfast."

We found a table in the cafeteria where we could talk privately.

"I'm sure you've read everything you could find about head injuries, Mom, so fill me in. Start with good, to bad, to baddest." I grinned, trying to bolster her much-too-serious mood.

"You're right, Bobby, I have. And Dr. Rosenblum gave me some extra material to read. The good news is that, with the shrapnel out, once the swelling in the brain goes down, the headaches will eventually go away. The bad is that he might be disoriented for a time and have some neurological issues."

"Neurological? What's that mean, Mom?"

"No one really knows. He could have speech problems or difficulty with balance and walking. His memory might take some time."

"Dad's always been sharp as a tack, Mom. His memory's been good since he came home."

"Well, some of it . . . with us. Dr. Rosenblum has spent a lot of time just talking to Dad. He says there are gaps in his memory from when his plane went down until he finally got to the hospital in England. According to Dr. Rosenblum, those may be experiences your Dad does not want to remember."

"So, are those the baddest?"

Mom bit her bottom lip and looked away. I kept my eye on her grasp on the cup. Her knuckles were white. "There is the possibility of neuroses."

"First, neurological. Now neuroses. More explanations—okay, Mom?"

She shook her head and gave me a bit of a smile. "That was a new word for me, too. Neuroses could be extreme anxiety, nightmares, unreasonable terror. Dr. Rosenblum says a lot of the veterans experience those. The brain is still quite a puzzle, it seems, even to doctors who study it. He mentioned a colleague of his in Vienna, a Dr. Freud." Mom smiled at the memory. "I guess they got into some lively discussions, though some might call them arguments."

"But he can help Dad through that stuff, can't he?"

Mom reached for my hand. "Remember when he told us our job was to be patient and encouraging? I think he meant *to be prepared for anything.* You and I will simply think positively. Let's go see if Dad is awake."

CHAPTER 21

PATH TO RECOVERY

We made our way back toward Dad's room. Hospital staff moved quietly, conversing in whispers. We did the same and stopped outside his open door. Morning light was slanting through the window and falling across the foot of his bed. Dr. Rosenblum was examining Dad's eyes; then he seemed to test the grip in his fingers. Dad mumbled something I couldn't make out. Seeing us waiting, the doctor motioned us in.

Mom hurried to Dad's bedside and grasped his hand. She leaned over and planted a kiss on his bandaged head. "Morning, Sweetheart," she said into his ear. I pulled two chairs over for us to sit.

Dr. Rosenblum nodded a greeting to us as he continued checking Dad out. Try as I might, I could never figure out if we're going to get good news, bad news, or no news at all. He explained what the tests revealed so far, and then, he got up to leave. As he walked past me, he tapped me on the shoulder and motioned to the hall.

Mom was holding Dad's hand between her own and never noticed me slip out of the room. Dr. Rosenblum guided me into a small room and motioned to a chair. What news did he have for me—and away from Mom? My heart began to thump, and my hands got sweaty.

The doctor smiled at me. "It's okay, Bobby. This is a scary time for you and your mom. Your father is doing as well as can be expected, but he has a long recovery ahead. I think he will do better if we can get him home, and I can visit him there."

My body about collapsed with relief. *My Dad was coming home!*

He noticed my reaction and held up his hand. "But not quite yet. He still needs physical therapy here for speech, balance, and walking. And I want to do some other therapy with him to help with his nightmares. Those would frighten your mother, I'm afraid." He leaned back in his chair and wiped his glasses with a handkerchief. "I may try hypnotism, which I learned from my colleague, Dr. Freud. I hope it will help him face the worst of his experiences. It has been an effective treatment with others—and it won't hurt him."

"Wow, Dr. Rosenblum. I thought hypnotism was just for magic shows."

"Well, I suppose it may have some entertainment value, but it can be useful for cases of panic and trauma. My guess is that your dad's nightmares stem from his mind not wanting to cope with what he went through. So, then those experiences surface as nightmares. He'll be able to move forward once those are dealt with."

"Thanks for helping him, Dr. Rosenblum. Is there anything I or my Mom can do to help?"

"He's calmer when your Mom is here. Are you okay being on your own a bit more?"

"I'm fine on my own, though Mom fusses some." I rolled my eyes, and Dr. Rosenblum smiled at me. "My friend Don lives across the street, and his parents let him stay with me. He's at my house right now, taking care of Sarge."

"Is Don's last name McDowell?"

I nodded.

"Yes, I know his father."

This should not have been a surprise. The military was an endless web of networks.

Dr. Rosenblum stood. "Come walk with me."

Along the way, I noticed the quiet movements of staff in and out of patient rooms. Other family members hovered around, concerned expressions on each face. Like Mom and me.

We reached a different part of the hospital and entered a large area. Staff members were working with several patients—some walking between bars, others using weights and pulleys.

"Wow, what is all this?"

"This is our physical-therapy center, where we help patients to recover their balance and strengthen their muscles. It can be a long process, and often painful and exhausting. But they all want to go home and hope to be able to care for themselves." He looked over his wire-rimmed glasses at me. "Your dad will spend a lot of time here."

"Has he been here since his shoulder surgery?"

"No, that therapy is done in his room. I am concerned about his dizziness and disorientation after this last surgery."

Disorientation? Now there's a word I need to look up. Dr. Rosenblum noticed my puzzled look and explained. "His *confusion,* Bobby. Your dad is used to being in charge and making decisions and taking fast action. For now, we can't expect that of him. He needs rest and time to heal. Your mom is the best medicine in that area." He stopped outside a door. "But, let me show you this room."

We stood in the doorway. A man wearing thick glasses was seated in a chair. A white cane lay nearby. Across the room sat a dog with a trainer. "Say her name and motion her to "Come" and "Stay, Corporal."

"Ruby," the Corporal said. He motioned with his hand for the dog to "Come." The dog walked to him and stood. Then he raised a flat hand that told her to stay. He rubbed her ears and whispered to her.

Dr. Rosenblum nodded to the trainer, and we left the room. "We do not want to distract a working dog. That young soldier lost much of his eyesight. Ruby is going to help him be independent and keep him safe."

"Does the dog go with him when he leaves?" I asked.

"Oh, yes. He and Ruby are partners now."

"That is so cool, Dr. Rosenblum. I've been trying to train Sarge. I don't want him knocking Dad over and getting in the way." I smacked myself on the forehead. "I never thought to use hand signals. I always tell Sarge what I want."

"That's good, Bobby. Try combining hand signals with your voice for a time, and then just use your hand."

"Are there special signals for the different commands, like Sit and Stay?"

"Let me see what information I can dig up for you, Bobby." We halted outside Dad's room. "I'll have a word with your parents and then get on with my schedule."

Mom smiled as we entered. Dad still looked a bit foggy. After a few words, Dr. Rosenblum stood. We shook hands. I almost felt like a grown-up. "Now, go visit with your Dad."

CHAPTER 22

SARGE'S TRAINING

The van was crowded with several families going back to Ogden. Mom found a place for herself, and I squeezed myself into the back seat with a bunch of younger kids. I wiggled myself into the middle to give my legs room to sprawl out into the aisle. A little girl grinned up at me as she swung her feet, unable to reach the floor.

I knew Mom wanted to talk about Dad's progress and prognosis during the trip. Yet I was happy to have this travel time to plan my workouts with Sarge. I wanted him to be perfect with every command I gave. I imagined Dad grinning at how well he would perform. How long would it be before he came home and we were together again? When I saw his bandages and thought about the surgeries he's had, my own hands and feet tingled, and the tips of my fingers hurt. My

Dad was a war hero, and I was so proud of him. The best was knowing he would be home this summer.

Then my thoughts turned to Arnie and what I'd seen at his house. Was his dad really involved in the Black Market? While my Dad is shot down over France, Arnie's dad is stealing gas! My whole body stiffened. The little girl next to me moved away and gave me a frightened look.

I relaxed and smiled at her. "It's okay."

"You looked really mad."

"Yes, I am, but not at you. Just some bad guy."

She nodded. "I get mad, too. Some bad soldier shot my dad. Today was a good day. I got to snuggle next to him." She moved back toward me and began humming.

I went back to thinking about Arnie's dad. How could I find out if he was into the Black Market? And what could I do about it? Would anyone believe me? Then I thought about my Scout troop. Don and I still helped with scrap drives and worked with the younger boys. Would our Scout master have any information about those underhanded dealings? It had to be illegal.

I was planning another venture to Arnie's neighborhood, when the van stopped at the corner to let folks out. As Mom and I walked to our house, she laced her fingers through mine and squeezed. Her eyes twinkled as she looked up at me.

"Dad looked good, don't you think, Bobby? Dr. Rosenblum is pretty sure he will make a full recovery. Of course, it will take time." She paused at our gate. "He wants me to spend more time at the hospital to keep Dad focused on what he needs to do. I don't like leaving you . . .

"Mom, what's going to happen to me? I have Sarge. No one is going to mess with that dog. The McDowells and Fletchers take turns feeding me. I've even learned to scramble eggs and fix cold cereal."

That made her laugh. "Well, I'll share ration stamps with Angie and Anna. I'm sure they will be happy to get them. And, I'll stock up on cereal and milk . . . and eggs. I might even leave my recipe file on the counter."

▲ ▲ ▲

Monday, after school, Mom marched me to the grocery store with her to learn the intricacies of buying with ration stamps and where items were located. This was new territory for me. I promised to keep myself, and Don, well supplied so that I didn't depend on being fed. She caught the van Tuesday to go be with Dad after I made a hundred or so promises to take care of myself, Sarge, and the house, and not to be a burden.

Before Don came over to spend Tuesday night with me, I made a list of what I would do while I was on my own. First would be Sarge—brushing him, walking him after school to wear him out a bit, and then his training. I hoped to add in hand signals. Next would be spying at Arnie's place, after dark. I was sure Don would join me and Sarge. Then, I had to learn about the Black Market. Scouts was this coming Friday. I'd find a way to bring it up. I don't even know who is in charge of that sort of thing. What happens to someone who is caught?

Hung at daybreak, perhaps?

CHAPTER 23

SARGE AND WHAT'S THE BLACK MARKET?

After school, Don would check in at his house, and I would give Sarge a snack and ready him for a walk. Tired of puppysitting himself all day, he was more than ready to walk his boys. He would wiggle his back end, prance at the gate on all four paws, and off we would go.

Spring was doing its best to make an entrance. The receding snow left grass and mud in its wake. Don and I wore boots for these outings, but Sarge paid no mind to where he ran, walked, or splashed. If he could have yipped for joy, he would have. His exuberance was contagious, and we started throwing sloppy snowballs at him and each other.

After an hour or so, we headed home with a more docile dog.

"Mom had lots of vegetables and chicken left over from the one she roasted Sunday, so she's making chicken pot pie tonight," Don said. "She'll call or send Sharon to get us."

"My bet is it will be Sharon. She likes bossing the big boys around."

While Sarge gobbled his supper, I explained to Don what I had observed in the hospital therapy rooms. "Let's use both signals with Sarge and see how it goes," Don suggested. "Do you want me to hold him on the other side of the yard?"

We worked with my dog for a while. Don held his collar and quieted him down. I called his name, said "Come" and beckoned him to me. When he got to me, I said "Stay" and held up a hand, palm out. After half a dozen times, Sarge seemed to like this new game with his two boys. A knock at the front door told us Sharon had arrived. I gave my dog a treat and left him stretched out on his rug in my room. We followed Sharon's march across the street.

Supper is always a great time with the McDowells. Then I thought how nice it would be to get Dad home and enjoy our own family dinners. Don's parents both asked about Dad's surgeries and how he and Mom were doing. I remembered to thank them for feeding me and lending Don out.

Just before Don and I left for my place, the phone rang. Mr. McDowell talked a few minutes, hung up, and clapped his hands. "Hurray for the good guys. Seems some Black Marketeers were nabbed red-handed. Sleazy bums."

Don saw the opportunity. "Dad, would you explain the Black Market to us? I hear the word on the radio, even in the movies, but I don't understand what it is."

Mr. McDowell tilted his head as he considered what to tell. "I guess it's a good thing for you to know. Just don't act like you know too much at school. The Black Market is a criminal operation, where people are trying to make a fast buck. When there are shortages, some folks try to fill the gaps at a higher price. These could be stolen food items, ration stamps that might be stolen or counterfeit, gasoline, or tires. The Black Market is an underground movement to supply illegal goods for an inflated price. And some people will pay it."

"Are these just ordinary people who do this?" I asked.

"I guess you could call them ordinary, up to a point. But they get sucked into it, and then they are criminals."

"While my Dad gets shot down overseas and spends months in the hospital, others are getting rich on the Black Market." Again I could feel anger tighten my muscles and knew it showed on my face. "These guys who were caught—what happens to them?"

"The OPA, Office of Price Administration, is in charge of that. People who are caught could spend a year in jail and pay a fine of up to $5000. They try to be tough on them to discourage others. It's not easy to catch these rascals. They are secretive and operate in the shadows. They almost have to be nabbed red-handed."

This news gave me a lot to think about. I knew where some of this was happening, but what do I do about it? Don saw the wheels in my brain kicking into gear and decided it was time for us to skedaddle. "Come on, Bobby. Time for us to have a bowl or two of cereal before bedtime."

His mom shook her head. "And I thought I just fed you two."

CHAPTER 24

MORE ABOUT SARGE AND ARNIE

Sarge was full of energy, as well as of himself. Yet, if we were going to do training, he had to learn to calm down. He was catching on to *come, to me* and *stay*, but getting him to *heel* was a challenge.

"Let's just walk him a bit and let him stretch his legs," Don said.

Sarge had no problem with *come*. He was already wiggling in front of me, but I gave the command anyway while pointing to myself. He was not inclined to *stay* as I put the leash on, so I forced his rear down. Don was laughing.

As we headed up the hill, I didn't even try to hold him back, as he watered every weed and post along the way. I tossed his ball half a dozen times; then I clicked the leash on him again, with him on my left. I showed him the flat of my hand, "Down." He wagged his tail and tilted his head at me. "Down," I repeated as I pushed his rear with the flat of my hand. He licked my hand before he lay down. "Good dog." I rubbed his ears. I tugged his leash straight up and commanded, "Heel." We walked forward, and he stayed with me on my left. Don watched silently. I kept repeating *heel*. When I flattened my hand, he lay down before I said the word.

Receiving cheers and ear rubs from both his boys, plus a treat from my pocket, he was the proudest German shepherd in the state.

Sarge caught on fast once he associated the command words with the hand signals. He just needed his exercise time first. Then we got down to business. Don wanted to give him a try. At first, Sarge gave me an "Is this okay?" look; then he accepted the commands and signals from Don.

On the days Don stayed with his family until almost bedtime, I alternated play time with training episodes to reinforce what Sarge had learned. Those evenings, I'd have cereal or peanut butter sandwiches. Sarge lapped up the milk in the bowl and rolled crusts of a sandwich around his tongue. He seemed to expect an endless supply of both. I showed him empty hands. "All gone." He caught on to that, too, but not willingly.

▲ ▲ ▲

A schedule evolved. Mom caught the van on Thursdays after I left for school, and I traveled to the hospital on Saturdays. It seemed like she finally realized I was fifteen and could manage on my own. I kept up with my schoolwork, and Arnie had not sabotaged my workshop project any further. However, the scene I'd observed with Arnie's dad played in my mind. Was he part of the Black Market? Seemed like it to me. A closer look was in order.

Don was babysitting Sharon again, so I walked Sarge down to Arnie's neighborhood. Jay came out to meet Sarge, so I demonstrated the commands he knew.

"Pretty cool," Jay said. "He's a nice dog. It seems the only German shepherds I've seen are in the movies. You know—the ones Nazis threaten people with." He shrugged. "I guess any dog will do what it's taught to do."

This seemed a good time to bring up Arnie. "Tell me, Jay. Do you have any idea why Arnie is afraid of dogs?"

"How so?"

"Well, a few weeks back I was exercising Sarge up in that field and spied Arnie up there. When he saw Sarge, he turned around and split."

Jay thought a bit. "I've lived near his family a long time. I do remember a farmer friend of Mr. Larsen's stopping by, with his big dog in the back of his pickup. Arnie was pretty young then. So was I. Anyway, Arnie tried to climb up on the bumper to see the dog. It was protective of the truck; he barked and curled his lip. It scared the dickens out of Arnie. He screamed and ran for the house. I was out in my yard, and all that scared me, too. We must have been only four or five."

"Wow! Was the dog vicious?"

"I don't think so. Just protecting the farmer's truck. But get this. Arnie's dad laughed and grabbed Arnie. Took him back to where the dog was. He thrust Arnie up to the dog, who barked and growled. He did it over and over again. Then he laughed when Arnie peed his britches, and called him a 'scaredy cat.' I don't think the farmer thought it was funny, as the two men had words."

I visualized the scene and knew right then I did not like Mr. Larsen. If he was into the Black Market, he deserved to be caught. But how?

CHAPTER 25

Dad and His Therapies

Saturday morning, I secured Sarge in the backyard with plenty of water and food. Don would come over later to walk him, feed him, and stay the night. I hated leaving Sarge, but I needed to see Dad, too.

The van ride was boring by now, but I was glad it was available. Mom was watching for me. She smiled, but her eyes looked troubled.

"What's going on, Mom? Is there a problem with Dad?"

She hooked her arm in mine as if it were a life raft. "I'm glad you're here. Dr. Rosenblum seems to think Dad is improving, but there have been setbacks. That's when I get upset." Tears floated in her eyes. She dabbed at them. "Bobby, I just want to get him home and us to be a family again."

We turned down a hall. "His room is the second one. He's waiting for you."

He sure was. His wheelchair was posted just inside the door as if he were waiting for the starting gun in a race.

"Hey, son. Ready to bust me out of this room?" He pushed himself into the hall as well as he could with one good arm. "Let's go to the cafeteria. No doubt you're hungry."

I pushed the wheelchair up to a table. "Not here, Bobby. Would you move me around so I can look out the window? I love the mountains."

Dad fired one question after another—about Sarge, Don, school and, finally, about Arnie. I did my best to fill him in. Mom excused herself for a few minutes. This was my chance.

"So, Dad, how is it *really* going? I can tell Mom is worried, but she won't say why. Are you getting physical therapy? What's Dr. Rosenblum doing to help you sleep?"

Dad grinned. "Your mom won't be gone long, so I better talk fast. Yes, I'm getting therapy, and those can be rough sessions. They call them ROM, range of motion. All those weeks of not using that arm must have frozen my joints. And here I thought it was from being so cold so long. Look." He raised his arm up and around to demonstrate. "And, I have a rubber ball I'm supposed to squeeze twenty times every two hours. Those do make my arm and hand tired."

"And, how about . . . ?" I pointed to his head. "The bandage is smaller. Are you sleeping any better?"

Dad leaned across the table. "It's coming, but it's slow. Imagine, if you can, Bobby, being scared, threatened, hurting, cold and hungry—plus, you're in a POW camp. And, yes, I was scared." As he spoke, his eyes first grew intense and then haunted. He gazed out at the mountains as if he were someplace else for a moment. "Of course, I wasn't the only one. It was that military camaraderie, or brotherhood, for lack of a better word, that held us together and able to face each day. I doubt your mom can even visualize what it was like—and I don't want her to."

He sat back and searched the mountains as if he could see that POW camp thousands of miles away. "I knew young men, not much older than you, facing challenges way beyond their years. And, Bobby, I think, and I dream about those I left behind, and I wonder . . . Dr. Rosenblum is helping me sort some of that out. I don't want to carry it home with me." His face brightened. "Before long, maybe the three of us can spend an evening, and I can tell you all that happened, when I have a better handle on it myself."

I looked over at the doorway. "Mom's on her way back, Dad. She's chatting with one of the nurses."

Dad glanced over his shoulder. "Dr. Rosenblum sometimes meets with me alone, so I imagine your mom is feeling a bit excluded. Think I'll have her come to the physical therapy sessions, so she will know what to nag me about when I get home."

Mom pulled out her chair. "What is this you're plotting, Buzz?"

"Just telling Bobby I'm planning on having you join me exercising in the gym, honey. We'll lift barbells together."

I grinned as I visualized that. This was *my Dad* back again, teasing. Yet, I looked forward to hearing about all that had happened to him *over there.*

CHAPTER 26

WHAT TO DO NEXT?

Mom and I enjoyed Sunday again with Dad, but I did notice his mood swings. For a time he was happy and excited, and then it was as if he'd left us and gone *somewhere else* we couldn't follow. He napped in between, but we all enjoyed our meals together.

While Mom checked on the van's arrival, I had a few minutes with Dad alone.

"Are you managing okay on your own, Bobby? It's great to have your Mom here, but we both worry about you."

"Dad, I couldn't be in a better place. You concentrate on getting yourself home, and I will be there waiting for you. Me and Sarge both. Mom needs to be here with you. We'll be a family, together, again, soon. Dr. Rosenblum says he can continue to see you there, too." Ruth flashed through my mind. "Uh, has he mentioned much about his family to you?"

"Not much," Dad said. "I know he and his daughter helped Sarge when he was shot. And I see her a bit at the hospital with him. Is there a problem?"

I filled him in a bit about that family's difficult situation. "Maybe when you are home, we could invite Dr. Rosenblum and Ruth over from time to time—not for doctor stuff—more to just enjoy a good time. I don't think they have anyone in this country."

"That's an excellent idea, Bobby. We will certainly do that. You answered some questions I had about him and his daughter." He grinned and gave me a knuckle. "I don't always think just about my own issues."

Mom appeared. "The van's loading, Bobby. Time to go." She hugged Dad and kissed his bandaged head. "See you day after tomorrow."

▲ ▲ ▲

The van was crowded, as usual. Folks were glad to have this service, what with the gas and tire rationing. I sat in the back with the kids and found that same little girl sitting next to me. She smiled up at me, swinging her feet as I stretched my legs out.

I was eager to see Sarge again and get back to his training. *Had Don done any with him while I was gone? Yeah, I bet he did*, and smiled to myself.

"You look happy today," the girl said. "I'm happy, too. I think my daddy knew I was there with him."

Her words sort of shook me up. "No wonder you're smiling. Was he hurt badly?"

"Yes, some bad soldier shot him in the war. Mama says we need to be thankful he is home and getting better." She leaned closer as if telling me a secret. "You know what? When mama left the room to go to the bathroom, I climbed on the bed to snuggle with daddy, like we used to do. I sang our song to him, too. He rolled over to me and hugged me. He knew I was there." She twisted her little fingers around and looked up at me. "And, you know what else? Mama let me stay there. She said daddy was smiling."

She began humming a little tune as I thought how lucky I was that Dad knew I was there, even if his thoughts wandered at times. This was a huge hospital, and every patient in it was a hero. I felt such pride in my Dad; then I thought of Arnie's dad avoiding service and stealing gas. The more I thought about it, the more convinced I was he was in the Black Market. I would find a way to expose him—I just couldn't think how.

CHAPTER 27

MEANWHILE BACK AT . . .

While I was at school Monday and Tuesday, Mom got all our laundry done and marched me again to the store. Mrs. McDowell had invited us over for dinner Tuesday evening, and Mom put together a cobbler to take. The surprise was that Laura Ann and her family joined us. I looked forward to Dad meeting both families. I figured he and these other two dads would find lots to discuss.

Mom, I know, enjoyed chatting with other grown-ups, Jackie and Sharon escaped to do whatever six-year-olds do, and Laura Ann, Don, and I lazily played cards, but mostly talked. She was assistant editor of the school newspaper now and hoped to write an article about training dogs, like Sarge. I knew we could expect her to show up at our training sessions.

"Is Sarge completely recovered from the gunshot wound, Bobby?"

"Oh, yeah, he's good. He's really grown a lot since then."

"He sure has," Don said. "He's a big dog, and smart, too. We have to wear him out some before he can get down to his training routine."

Laura Ann laughed. "Does he wear you two out at the same time?"

Don elbowed me. "Tell her about running into Arnie up in the field . . . with his dad's rifle."

She listened to my story. "But why is Arnie so afraid of your dog, Bobby?"

"I don't think it's just Sarge. I think it's all dogs." And I repeated what Jay had told me about how Arnie's dad terrorized him with a dog when he was a little guy.

"That's horrible," Laura Ann said. "What kind of dad would do that? Arnie was probably about Jackie's age."

"Maybe younger, according to Jay. I saw that creep one evening. He is not a nice man."

Before we knew it, Laura Ann knew everything we knew about dogs and the Black Market. "Wow," she said. "You guys have given me lots of ideas to write about. Dog training, the Black Market, and the military hospital. There are tons of things my readers do not know about. Thanks."

Don and I looked at each other. Had we just opened a can of worms?

▲ ▲ ▲

Mom caught the van to the hospital the next morning, but not before giving me detailed instructions as I shut Sarge safely in the backyard. I saluted her, grinned, and said, "Yes, Sir . . . uh, Ma'_yum," over and over as I marched backward to the gate."

She was laughing when I joined Don to walk to school.

"It's great to see your mom happy, Bob," Don said. "She's like a different person, compared to this time last year."

"You know, Don, I think she was afraid the whole time that Nazi lived upstairs. I tried to make sure I was here whenever he might be. It was just a weird time."

"I doubt he would have hurt your mom. That would have blown his cover. Now, Laura Ann!" He smacked his forehead. "That's a different matter!. She knew just how *to poke the bear*. He would have loved wringing her neck." We both laughed recalling how that all had gone down. We didn't joke much back then.

▲ ▲ ▲

During woodshop, I put the second coat of paint on the birdhouse and listened to Arnie make excuses about his gun rack.

"Mr. Swanson, I did measure—twice. You can still see both pencil lines."

Our teacher had the patience of Job when it came to that guy. "But, Arnie, which one did you mean to cut? This is not going to fit evenly."

Arnie screeched his stool over the concrete floor. "I did it right! Either that saw is dull, or it cuts crooked."

Mr. Swanson handed him several sheets of rough sandpaper. "That saw can't fix it now, Arnie, but sandpaper and elbow grease will even that edge."

"Aw, Mr. Swanson, can't I just cut another piece?"

"Nope, three's the limit. You can make it work. Just don't take too much off."

Arnie saw the smile on my face. "What'cha laughing at, Bradley? My dad's coming home tonight, so don't get cute."

I had no idea what that threat meant, but I doubt he did, either. Arnie talked big and was a real pain, but still I felt sorry for him. His dad? That was different.

▲ ▲ ▲

While Don checked in at home, I slurped a bowl of cereal to sustain me. The soup Mom left could wait until later. I gave Sarge a treat and clicked on his leash. The three of us set off to do some training.

"You did some good work with him, Don. He's connecting the verbal and hand signals better."

"I got an idea, Bob. Let's teach him to salute. Wouldn't your dad love that?"

"Great idea!" I could visualize my dog saluting my Dad. "He already shakes hands and sits and lifts both paws. Do you think he would imitate us if we say *Salute* and saluted him?"

"Sounds good. But, let's wear him out a bit now."

We played with Sarge and went through all his training. He watched us as if this were a game, and he tried to anticipate what his signal might be. Yet when we said *Salute* and saluted him, Sarge just cocked his ears and wagged his tail.

CHAPTER 28

IMPROVEMENT

Weeks passed. My Dad steadily improved. One weekend, he said, "Dr. Rosenblum and I had a long talk. He thinks I could go home soon and continue my recovery there. It seems, one day a week, he visits his patients in Ogden." He beamed. "One of them will be me."

Mom squealed, and her face lit up. "Oh, Buzz, it will be so good to get you home with us. I've prayed for this every day." She kissed him, ruffled his hair, and kissed him again. Dad, who sported only a small bandage on his scalp, even blushed a bit.

I felt myself grinning all over. "Wow, Dad, when do you think that will happen? How will you get there?"

"Whoa," Dad said. "There's both military and medical paperwork involved, so it won't happen tomorrow." He suddenly got serious. "But I think it's time I filled you two in about getting shot down and all that happened before I arrived at the hospital here. Dr. Rosenblum believes I'm ready to work through that with you. I've arranged for us to share dinner and have time to talk. Let's head down there now." Then he stood straight up, put an arm around each of us, and walked us to the cafeteria. No wheelchair, no cane—just the three of us.

After dinner, we found a small lounge area where we could talk. If I closed my eyes, it was like watching a war movie, as Dad told his story. He left out nothing—how frightened he was when his plane went down, the treatment and threats of the Nazi Gestapo, his interrogation at the POW camp, and the friends he made there. His eyes filled with tears as he remembered the British medic who was so kind to him. "I hope he makes it out safely," he murmured.

I could see him relive his escape with two other pilots, led by a string of French Resistance fighters—the cold, the hunger, the danger, and, always, the pain from his shoulder and his head. I could almost feel the waves of the English Channel slapping against the gunboat amidst the strafing of the German planes. His tension faded as he talked about the relief and peace of being safe and cared for in the Plymouth hospital. Mom and I sat quietly, letting him talk and talk.

At length, he took a deep breath. "I'm glad to finally share all of that with you, but it's behind us now. Maybe, one day,

I will write it all down. Right now, I just want to get home with my family."

All three of us had tears, but they were happy ones.

CHAPTER 29

Dangerous Confrontation

With Dad due to arrive home soon, I stepped up my walks with Sarge and intensified his training. We used only hand signals now, with an occasional voice command. But he still simply flicked his ears and flopped his tail when we said *Salute* as we saluted him.

"You'd think by now he'd have caught onto saluting," Don complained. "We've been doing it for days."

"I dunno. He's good with all the other commands." I punched his arm. "Maybe we don't look like officer material, and he's picky."

Don laughed. "I'm getting hungry. Let's head back."

"Can you hold out a bit longer? It's almost dusk and a good time to sneak in a visit over Arnie's way. Maybe you'll get to see what I've seen."

Don grasped his throat and stomach and staggered around. "I'll try not to keel over from starvation before we head home."

Don's stockier than I am. I pinched his middle roll. "You'll survive. Let's go."

Sarge obediently trotted on my left, which put him between the two of us. We met Jay, having just earned his driving license, as he pulled into his driveway. He greeted us and rubbed Sarge's ears. "Need your phone number again, Don. Lost it. I'll write it on my notebook this time." He jotted it down and pointed the pencil at Don as he spoke to me. "*He* understands the mysteries of trigonometry way better than me."

The sound of a truck shifting gears to back into a driveway interrupted us.

"Uh, oh!" Jay said. "Looks like the local bully is home again to keep the neighborhood in an uproar. My dad called the cops last week. He not only threatened Arnie—he also yelled at the mom and even the sister. It got ugly."

"What's he got to get upset about? All he does is drive a truck." I popped a couple knuckles.

"I dunno. Maybe it's not going well, and he's afraid he'll get drafted after all," Jay said. "My dad's number came up again, but he's a supervisor out at the parachute plant. Doubt they'll call him, but you never know. Women filling in those jobs now. Thanks for the number." The door slammed behind him.

I knelt on the sidewalk by my dog and watched Mr. Larsen stomp around his truck. He yelled and popped Arnie on the back of the head. A growl rumbled out of Sarge's throat.

Reaching to pet him, I found the hackles on his neck on high alert. I put my hand around his muzzle to quiet him and nudged Don. "Let's sneak down into the vacant lot. There's a rock and some brush we can hide behind." I pointed. Don followed.

Mr. Larsen flicked on their garage light, yelling to Arnie to watch as he backed the tanker closer.

"What's Arnie lugging out?" Don whispered.

"Gas cans. Watch what happens now, Don."

Looking as if he were already about to gag, Arnie stretched out the length of hose and stuck it into the tanker. Right then, I felt so sorry for him.

"He's not making Arnie drink the stuff, is he?"

"Not quite," I said. "Watch."

The dad climbed out of the truck, popped Arnie's head again, and yelled.

Sarge tensed and growled.

Just then, everything went sideways. Arnie tried to suck, got sick, and threw up all over the driveway, the tanker, himself, and then his dad. Mr. Larsen snatched the length of suction hose from the ground, using it as a whip to beat his son.

Arnie screamed; Don and I both stood up.

Sarge did better than us. He jerked his leash out of my hand and raced through the brush. With a bark and a growl, he launched himself at Mr. Larsen's raised arm.

Mr. Larsen swung the hose wildly, but now at my dog. Dodging this whip Sarge turned, planted his feet, bared his fangs and waited. Larsen's arm was bleeding, his face crimson with fury as he again swung at Sarge. The dog yelped.

Jay must have heard the commotion and came out of his house. I could hear Don yell something to him. I rushed to help my dog.

I stood between Sarge and Arnie's dad. That's when I realized how huge Mr. Larsen was. I looked back at Sarge. He was ready to attack again, lip curled to reveal those dangerous fangs.

"Stop," I yelled. "Stay, Sarge!" He blinked but kept his eyes on the man standing over us.

"That your dog, Sonny? Ya know I'm going to kill him, don't ya?"

Arnie spoke out of the shadows. "Don't, Dad!"

Larsen turned on his son. "What do you know? You're such a sissy. Watch. You might learn something."

I looked at Sarge. Waves of fear flowed over me—for Sarge, for me, for Arnie. Why had I brought Sarge this close? Those deep growls and raised hackles never left him as we'd crouched behind that rock. Now every muscle trembled as he kept his eyes fixed on the man.

Larsen was whipping that hose around, ignoring blood from the bite wounds sprinkling the driveway. He glanced over at Arnie and laughed.

I looked at Sarge. Would he know what to do? I yelled the command. "Go, Sarge!"

He launched himself at Arnie's dad, hitting him smack in the chest and knocking him backward. Feet planted on his chest, Sarge stood over him, growling, teeth snapping the air. I ran in and jerked the hose from Larsen's hand. His face pale now, he rolled his eyes at me. His trembling hands covered his throat and face. "Call him off."

Sirens wailed, coming closer. I looked down at Mr. Larsen, and then at Sarge. "Stay!" I ordered—to both of them.

Jay had called not only the police but also Don's dad. Sarge had plenty of help now. The messy scene in the driveway, on the truck, as well as on Arnie and his dad pretty much told the tale. I handed Mr. McDowell the piece of hose as we described what we had observed.

An officer tended the bite on Mr. Larsen's arm, assuring him he would get treatment for rabies. Knowing how painful that series of shots is, Mr. Larsen began blaming that *dangerous* dog for giving him rabies. The officer looked over at Sarge, now lying by my feet, tongue lolling out, and tail beating the ground. "I doubt you're in any danger—but just to be sure, we'll have you checked out at the station."

Mr. McDowell walked over. "You keep him right there. I want to question him, and I'm sure the OPA guys will, too. I hear there's too much Black Marketeering going on with gasoline these days."

Mr. Larsen turned pale all over again.

"Bring your dog, boys. I'll give you a ride home. Sarge is favoring that leg again."

He dropped us off at my house. "You have something to eat—besides cereal, I mean?"

"Yes, sir," I said. "Mom left a pot of soup in the fridge. I know how to turn on the stove now."

"Good enough," he said and gave us a thumbs-up. "And good job."

Inside, I put the soup on and then got on the floor to check Sarge out. He did wince as I ran my fingers over his left rib cage. Then Sarge licked my fingers as if to say, "I think that soup is ready."

All three of us slurped soup as Don and I replayed what had happened.

Don dipped a cracker in his soup. "No wonder Arnie's so big. Look at the size of his dad. Weren't you just a little bit scared?"

"Yep, lots!" I admitted with a shudder. "But I couldn't leave Sarge at that point, and he sure wasn't backing down."

"How do you think Sarge knew what to do?"

"I've been thinking about that myself. It was a Captain Jamison who gave him to me. I think he was an MP. Maybe Sarge was being trained for defensive and offensive work from the start."

"Sarge was pretty young. Do you think maybe he watched older dogs being trained and remembered?"

"Could be, I suppose." I sat down with my third bowl of soup and pointed to the stove. "Have some more, Don." I crumbled crackers into mine. "All I know is that Sarge was poised to attack. So, I said *Go* and pointed. Caught Larsen by complete surprise, and down he went."

Don hooted. "Boy, didn't he? He didn't know what hit him."

"I think Sarge weighs close to eighty pounds now, and he's fast."

We were both proud of our dog—now stretched out on the couch, where he was not supposed to be.

CHAPTER 30

WHAT ABOUT ARNIE?

Don and I replayed the scene with Arnie's dad as we walked to school. Everything had happened so fast: the dad backing his truck in, smacking Arnie on the back of his head, Arnie getting sick, and his dad becoming violent. I thought about Sarge growling, hackles up, eyes fixed on the scene below.

"You know, Don," I said. "Sarge was so ready to attack, but he waited for my command. All our training paid off."

"Mr. Larsen would have beat Arnie with that hose if Sarge hadn't launched at him. Did you see how red in the face he got when he realized he'd been bitten? I really think he was ready to kill Sarge."

"He said as much." I shuddered.

"Then he would have started on you, Bob."

"Yeah. And, silly me, I thought I could calm him down." I wiped my brow. "Big mistake. The only thing I could do was tell Sarge to go for it."

"Boy, didn't he!"

"Hey, you guys." Jay was waiting for us at the school steps. "That's some dog you have, Bobby. Larsen never knew what hit him."

"Did you see all that? Thanks for calling for backup, Jay. We needed it."

"Yeah, the cavalry got there just in time—like in the movies." Don imitated whipping out a pistol. "I'm glad you called my dad. He needed to be there, too."

"Has the neighborhood quieted down, Jay?"

He nodded. "Pretty calm at the Larsens'. No sign of Arnie, his mom, or the sister."

We separated for classes. I kept thinking about Arnie. What *did* happen in his family last night after everyone left? Was Arnie sad or relieved that his dad was hauled away? Don's dad said that Black Marketeering was a federal offense and that penalties are severe enough to send messages to other offenders. What would happen to Mr. Larsen?

▲ ▲ ▲

Arnie didn't show up at school until Friday. I found him waiting by my locker before shop class, head down, studying his shoes.

"Hi, Arnie," I said. "Been thinking about you. Must be hard."

He remained silent, but I saw his whole body tighten. Elbowing me, he motioned to the outside door and mumbled what sounded like "Go outside."

I wasn't sure I wanted to. Was Arnie angry at me for the trouble his dad was in? Would he take it out on me? Following him out the door, I figured I could always outrun him. I think.

He turned and plopped down at the top of the basement steps. Clasping his hands in front of his knees, he looked up at me. No meanness, no anger. "Is your dog okay, Bobby?"

"Uh, yeah, Arnie. Sarge's doing fine. He was hurt there before."

"Yeah, I know." He paused. "I did that. I thought he was a coyote. Guess I was just crazy ready to shoot whatever." He looked up at me, eyes glistening. "I'm really, really sorry."

I sat down next to him. "And how are things at your home, Arnie?"

He blew out a deep breath. "Bobby, you have no idea." Then he stopped and knocked himself on the side of his head. "No, *I* had no idea how really bad things were at my house. I guess we lived in fear. Everything was so tense when my dad was around. I think we forgot what *normal* could be like." He tilted his head sideways and smiled at me. "It's so peaceful. My mom is relaxed, even my sister. I'm glad about what happened the other night." He gave me an odd look. "Did you know what was going on?"

Oops! My turn to confess. So, I told him I had talked to Jay about him and learned how hard his dad was on him.

Then, I told him about walking Sarge to that neighborhood and seeing for myself. "It must have been awful, Arnie, having to siphon that gasoline. I felt so sorry for you."

He gave me an elbow and grinned. "Don't even think about trying it, Bob. It burns your throat, you gag, and you burp gasoline all night. It was my dad's idea of fun and games. I hate him for it and all his other mean stuff."

"Any idea what will happen to him, Arnie?"

"Well, they—whoever *they* are—want him to give the names of everyone he knows involved in Black Market gasoline. My mom went to see him, and he told her that he's no snitch. Mom thinks he's afraid of what the gang might do if he tells." Arnie shrugged. "I think he'll wind up in prison."

We sat side by side, each thinking his own thoughts. I never would have imagined that a month ago.

Arnie looked at me and spoke, with a bit of a grin on his face. "We're moving, Bobby. Goin' to my grandpa's farm in Idaho. I loved visiting there. Now I get to live there. I'll be going to a new school." He relaxed back on the step. "With my size, I 'spect they'll want me to go out for sports. But I'm tired of being the punchin' bag. I'm going to go out for band." His face lit up. "I love music. I'll be the best tuba player they ever heard."

I laughed. "I bet you will be, Arnie." I stood and slapped him on the shoulder. "I think we just missed most of shop class."

We went down the steps and into the building just as the bell rang. Mr. Swanson opened his classroom door and looked at us over his glasses. "I marked you two boys as excused absences."

I waited as Arnie emptied his locker. "That's about it, I guess," he said. "Won't need that ol' gun rack. Grandpa has one."

"Good luck to you, Arnie, and enjoy that tuba."

"One more thing, Bobby. Grandpa's coming with his truck and hay trailer the end of next week. Would you have time to bring Sarge to my house? I've never liked being around dogs, but I would like to meet Sarge—like, for real."

"My Dad is supposed to come home from the hospital before long, Arnie. But I'll find you before you leave."

CHAPTER 31

Good Luck, Arnie

Mom climbed off the van Tuesday and all but danced her way home. "Bobby, Bobby! Dr. Rosenblum says Dad may get to come home this next week."

"That's great news! I talked with Dad last night, and he didn't say anything."

"Well, Bobby, you are to come back up with me this weekend, so that Dr. Rosenblum can explain to us what we can do or not do to help Dad in his recovery." Mom was so breathless that she could barely get the words out. "I don't understand which is which . . . but I guess he will tell us."

Mom's eyes were flitting from the curtains to the furniture to the carpet. "Oh, I should have been doing my spring cleaning over the past month" She threw up her hands. "How will I get it all done this week?"

147

"Oh, right, Mom." I stood before her with my hands on my hips and a grin on my face. "That's the big worry right now. Dad is sure to examine every speck of dust and wonder what you have been doing all these months. I can just hear Captain Bradley barking orders: 'Why hasn't that wife of mine scrubbed from floor to ceiling instead of riding a van up to the hospital every week? Twenty laps and 500 pushups for that military wife!'"

Mom caught her breath and stared at me. I shook my head. "He doesn't care, Mom, and you shouldn't, either. He just wants to be home. Bake him his favorite peach pie, and he won't notice any cobwebs or dust hanging around this house. And I will do my very best not to point it out. Scout's honor." I grinned at her.

She whipped her dish towel at me. "You tease just like your Dad does, Bobby Bradley!"

Then she hugged me and began to cry.

Uncertain about what was going on in this house, Sarge raised his paw at her and whined. She wiped at her eyes and knelt before him, rubbing his ears. "Sarge, he will be so happy to meet you. Thank you for babysitting Bobby while I was at the hospital." She sent a sly smile my way. "We both know how hard you had to work to make that boy behave."

Mom was teasing back in her own way, and I was happy to see her so light-hearted. Of course, she had no idea what Sarge and I had been up to in her absence. I'll 'fess up when

Dad is there to soften my story, or perhaps Major McDowell. Moms just naturally fuss too much.

I left Mom to her fussings. I had an obligation of my own to take care of this week. I whistled for Sarge. "Mom, I'm off to walk Sarge before those clouds dump rain or snow. Back in a bit."

I let Sarge run a bit in the field before I signaled him to *Come*, *Sit*, and *Stay* as I clipped on his leash. "Heel," I commanded, and off we went to Arnie's house.

▲ ▲ ▲

Sarge and I trotted through the empty lot to the Larsen driveway. There we found Arnie helping his granddad load items on a flatbed trailer. I noticed Sarge sniffing the air, probably checking for any sign of his adversary. Arnie saw us. His face lost color, and that look of fear took over at the sight of my dog. This wasn't surprising, as the last time he saw Sarge, this dog was snapping his fangs and slobbering in his dad's face.

"Hi, Arnie," I said. "Glad to see you're not making your grandfather do all the heavy work. We came over to wish you well."

He collected himself enough to introduce me to his grandfather and point out my dog. The granddad seemed to sense there was an issue here. "I'll go in and check with your mom, Arnie, to see what goes on next. You chat with your friend."

I plopped down on the curb with Sarge at my side. Arnie moved around to settle himself on the other side. "Thanks for coming over, Bobby . . . and you too, Sarge." He leaned forward as if to let my dog know he was included. He waved up at the load. "Didn't realize we had so much stuff. I'm glad for a break. My grandpa never slows down."

"You still lookin' forward to the move?"

"You bet!" Arnie was breathing easier but still tense. "My mom and sister are both so happy. S'pose we all need a new start." He was quiet a moment, sort of weaving his fingers around. I waited. "You know, Bobby—it's really strange."

"What's the problem, Arnie?"

"Not really a problem for us. But none of us seem to care what's goin' on with my dad. Mom just left his clothes and other stuff where he dropped it all. She says that's my dad's to sort out when he gets the chance." He was rocking back and forth now, and peeking over at Sarge. "Your dog doesn't look like the same dog who was here last week, Bobby."

Here was my chance. "You know, don't you, Arnie, that he was protecting you?"

"Me? Why would he do that? I'm the one who hurt him."

"He doesn't know that."

"No, I s'pose he don't. But he sure didn't like me when we met in the field."

"Think about it, Arnie. You were threatening me then, and he sensed it. That's why his hackles went up and he growled." I motioned Sarge to move in front of me and sit as I rubbed his ears. "That night last week, Arnie, Don and I were walking my dog and stopped to chat with Jay. Then your dad started yelling at you and smacking you a bit. Sarge started that growl in his throat right then. We crept down into that lot, but, even then, Sarge was on alert."

"He was? I don't get it, Bobby, but then I don't know much about dogs."

"Dogs are about the most loyal friends you can have, Arnie. They are also sensitive to what's going on with the people around them. Sarge knew when you were sort of threatening me. But he really didn't like your dad threatening and slapping you around." I glanced sideways at Arnie. His eyes were fixed on the dog. "The louder your dad yelled, the more tense Sarge grew. His hackles stood on end, and that growl got even louder. When your dad grabbed that hose to beat you, Sarge surprised both me and Don when he launched himself at your dad's arm. And he wasn't about to back off then. He knew your dad was dangerous. I think he would have died protecting me and Don . . . and you."

Arnie's hand tentatively reached out to rub one of Sarge's ears, as I'd been doing. The dog turned and licked his fingers. "I think he likes me, Bobby."

About then, the grandpa trundled out with a huge box. "Grab the other end of this, son, will you? I'll be in trouble with your mom if I dump this on the pavement."

Arnie jumped up to help, and then turned to say good-bye. "Thanks for stopping over, Bobby, with Sarge. Will he let me touch him again?"

"He can do better than that." I pointed to Arnie. "Shake hands, Sarge."

Delighted, Arnie turned to his grandpa. "Did you see that, Pa? That dog's my friend."

The man chuckled. "We got a couple dogs on the farm who will be happy to have you and your sister around. Better stick with this loading, though, if we're going to leave in the morning."

"Bye, Arnie, and good luck. Enjoy your tuba."

He gave me a thumbs-up and waved.

On the walk home, I thought about Arnie and his family. They did deserve a new life. As for Mr. Larsen, I'm sure he, too, is facing a whole new future. No family, no job, no home. Would his misplaced loyalty to his gang of Black Marketeers land him in jail? And, with a huge fine, as Don's dad predicted? He seemed to be a big-time loser no matter what he chose.

When we reached our gate, I gave Sarge the hand signals to sit and stay. On a whim I said, "Salute," as I saluted him. He thumped his tail and waited for the gate to swing open.

CHAPTER 32

Receiving Instructions

Mom didn't go to the hospital this week, having her own mission to complete before Dad came home. She stirred up more dust than she evicted as she moved from room to room. Nothing I said changed her conviction that all must be *shipshape*. It was safer to just stay out of her way. But that didn't happen.

After school, I was pressed into service *cleaning the perimeter*. In plain English, I was on dog-poop detail. We were both in high spirits. Dad was coming home!

Saturday morning, Mom and I caught the van for what I assumed was our last trip to the hospital. Don volunteered to dog-sit with instructions from Mom to walk Sarge so he *did his business* elsewhere. He snapped her a salute, as I'd been doing.

▲ ▲ ▲

Mom laced her fingers with mine as we approached the hospital doors. "Oh, Bobby, there were times I thought this day would never come. It's been nineteen months since we've been a family."

"No, Mom," I said. "We've always been a family. From now on, we will be *living together* again like a normal family. Won't it be great waking up and just eating breakfast together? You've been so brave. I know you missed him just as much as I did."

She stopped me just inside the doors. "Bobby, you never gave up on your Dad when he was missing. Without you, I would have just fallen apart. I told your Dad that."

Fifteen-year-old guys don't get tears in their eyes, but I'm afraid this one did. Wordless, I gave her a hug, and we turned toward Dad's room.

He was sitting on the edge of his bed. A box of meds, bandages, and exercise devices lay beside him. Dr. Rosenblum stood up as we approached.

Mom hugged Dad. "Is he about ready for me to take him home, Dr. Rosenblum?" I squeezed Dad's hand and snagged two chairs for Mom and me.

The doctor nodded his head slowly. "I think so, or he would not be leaving. However, we need to talk about his care." He tilted his head toward Dad. "*He* is still in recovery, and you will have to outrank him in everything he does. He must do the exercises, eat properly, and sleep and nap, so that his body continues to heal. His surgeries have healed well, but the sites must be kept clean and covered to avoid infection."

He looked directly at Dad. "Captain Bradley, I do not want to readmit you, but I will if necessary."

I watched Dad's face. He nodded as if to a superior officer, one he respected.

Dr. Rosenblum handed Mom a folder. "In this is Buzz's exercise regimen and a suggested daily schedule. He must nap every day, even if you have to take one with him. Walking is good. He has a cane to use to reinforce his equilibrium. That head surgery was serious, and we can't have him falling, especially on that left shoulder I so carefully repaired." He smiled as Dad reached up to rub that arm. "There are phone numbers for you to call with any concerns. I have added my home number also." He stood. "I will leave the three of you to talk, but I will be back to borrow Bobby in an hour or so."

I watched him stroll away. *What would he want with me?*

Mom and Dad were holding hands as they planned his homecoming tomorrow. She giggled like a teenager. Dad couldn't take his eyes off her. Then they both reached for my hands to draw me in. Gave me shivers up my back and across my scalp. The best feeling in all the world is being together again. Mom and I filled Dad in on who was who in the neighborhood, plus how great a dog Sarge was.

Dr. Rosenblum appeared in the doorway and motioned for me. "I'll return him for lunch." We wound up in the physical-therapy area. "Let's watch the therapy dogs again, shall we?"

We stood in the doorway so as not to disturb the training-in-progress. I watched a black lab obey hand signals from a soldier with bandages over his eyes. The dog nuzzled his hand to let him know she was there. He spoke, "Good job, Lady."

After a time, we headed back toward Dad's room. Dr. Rosenblum looked over at me. "School will be out before we know it, Bobby. Do you have plans for the summer?"

"Not yet. I want to see how Dad gets along . . . if Mom needs any help. But I usually can find some sort of farm work."

"I have a suggestion. Would you be interested in bringing Sarge up here with you to help with the dog-training program? Our therapists are overwhelmed sometimes. I chatted with them to see if you and Sarge could give some relief. I'm sure the hospital would pay you."

"You mean I could help with the dog training?" I could hardly believe it. "And get paid to do it?"

Dr. Rosenblum chuckled. "I want to watch you work with Sarge first, but he sounds as if he's pretty smart. He's a fairly young dog, isn't he?"

"He won't be two until about next Christmas, but he's a really big dog already." I wanted to tell about him and Mr. Larsen, but I held back. Maybe later. "I would love to do something like that with him, but how would we get up here?"

"There is no problem that can't be solved, Bobby. Always remember that." He gave me a serious look and then tapped on the partially open door of Dad's room. "See, I return him in good shape, although he is probably hungry. May I join you in the cafeteria?"

Dad nodded. "Is this a test to see if I can handle being home, Dr. Rosenblum?"

"No, I'm sure you will do well. I want to talk about getting you home tomorrow. Besides, I'm hungry."

CHAPTER 33

THE HOMECOMING!

Sunday morning felt like Christmas when I was five years old. Butterflies flew from my stomach and fluttered in my chest. Ants crawled all over, and my fingers tingled. Mom looked like I felt. Dad did, too, as a matter of fact.

Per hospital protocol, Dad was wheeled out to Dr. Rosenblum's waiting car for the drive home. As the doctor left the parking lot, I said, "Wait, we forgot Ruth."

"No, she's already in town. She and her new friend Laura Ann are making cookies today with Mrs. Fletcher. It's good she gets to do girl things like that."

This was news to me, but I was glad the two girls had become friends. It was a gorgeous spring day, and, before long, we turned into our street. Dad was the first to speak. "It's been a long time, but isn't that our house? Who are all those people?"

Mom and I leaned forward to see. We hardly recognized the house. Balloons hung from the trees with a table set out below them. Chairs and blankets were strewn around the yard. A banner hung from the porch roof: "Welcome Home, Captain Bradley!" People smiled and waved as Dr. Rosenblum parked his car out front.

"Oh, Buzz, everyone has come to greet you. Isn't this wonderful?"

As Dad stepped out of the car to open the gate, everyone popped hats on their heads and stood to attention. It was almost too much to take in. All the kids wore *private* hats folded from newspapers; Mr. and Mrs. Fletcher wore white sailor hats; Major McDonald had a newspaper pirate's hat on, but Mrs. McDonald had a nurse's cap plus general epaulets on her shoulders. Even Dr. Rosenblum came around the car sporting a three-corner Napoleon hat. Don had Sarge sitting at his side, wearing my old aviator's cap.

At a signal, Jackie blew a whistle, and everyone saluted as we walked through the gate. I glanced over at Sarge, who was watching everyone salute. Guess he thought it was about time he got in the act also. He stepped forward, his ears pointed straight up, and he saluted, too.

Dad was speechless, Mom crying. What better welcome-home could any hero receive?

Don't think Don and I weren't just a bit proud of Sarge.

Dr. Rosenblum insisted Dad sit down under the tree, and Mom introduced everyone. After she went to help bring out the food, Don's and Laura Ann's dads dragged chairs close to Dad's, with one for Dr. Rosenblum. I spotted Ruth wearing a paper hat of some sort.

"So, you were in on all this, too?" I said, waving one hand around.

"Oh, yes, it was such fun. We made cookies, salads, and sandwiches. I must go now to help."

Don sidled over. "Pretty nice surprise, don't you think?"

"This is great, Don, but where's Sarge?"

"Where he thinks he is supposed to be, Bob—on duty." He pointed to the group of men. Sarge had wiggled his way in and had his chin resting on Dad's knee, as if this was what he had been waiting for. Dad was stroking him and rubbing his ears. What a picture!

Mom emerged with the other mothers, all carrying platters of sandwiches and pitchers of water and Kool-Aid. "Come and get it, and find a blanket to sit on," Midge McDowell called to everyone. "Cookies come later." She gave Sharon and Jackie warning looks.

"Think that was meant for us too, Don?" I said, as we joined the two girls under a different tree. "Thanks to all of you for doing this. Makes my Dad feel part of the group already."

Ruth touched Laura Ann's arm. "*Danke Schön, meine Freundin.*" They both giggled.

"Obviously, the *Deutsch* lessons are going well," Don said.

"I think what she said, Don, is that the boys are on KP duty," I said.

Ruth looked puzzled. "I do not know *KP duty*."

"You see, Ruth, that is something only girls are supposed to do." Don laughed as Laura Ann hit him with her paper hat.

"KP stands for Kitchen Police, Ruth. If you have that duty, you get to do the dirty dishes," Laura Ann said. "But, smart-aleck boys, we picked up these metal plates at the war surplus store, and the utensils. My mom and Don's mom will each take some home to wash up. They thought they would keep them for times like this. So, you, Don, may pull KP duty after all."

We were surprised to see Dr. Rosenblum stand up and bang on his plate for attention.

"This was a wonderful get-together, and I'm sure Buzz and Midge enjoyed every minute." He plopped his hat back on his head. "As Emperor Napoleon's distant cousin, I am assuming command. My patient has had enough excitement for today. Thanks to all of you."

Obediently, the crowd said their farewells and drifted off, carrying dirty dishes, chairs, and blankets. Mom had nothing left to do but hustle Dad inside to relax. Sarge escorted him, also, as if that were his newest duty. As rain clouds threatened, I gathered up anything left outside.

The three of us sat in the living room, happy and content. Sarge planted himself at Dad's feet.

"What a wonderful group of friends," Dad said. "Did you know they were planning this?"

"No," Mom said. "You didn't know either, did you, Bobby?"

"Nope." I stretched my legs out and leaned my head on the back of the sofa. "This is a lot different from a year ago, isn't it, Mom?"

"It certainly is, but that story is for another time." Dad looked puzzled, but she didn't explain. "Right now, Captain Bradley, it's time for your nap. Think I'll take one with you."

I stood up and looked at my dog. "If Sarge can tear himself away from your side, Dad, I think we will go for a quick walk before the rain hits."

Dad patted Sarge's head. "Go with Bobby, Sarge. There's no room for you on our bed."

CHAPTER 34

Lɪғᴇ Is Gᴏᴏᴅ

True to his word, Dr. Rosenblum stopped by the next week to check on Dad. He inspected the scars on his shoulder and his head, checked what is called ROM, or range of motion, for his shoulder, and the strength of his arm and hand. "You must keep up with those exercises, Captain Bradley. You are not quite to full strength yet."

Dad grinned at the doctor. "I will stick with them if you will begin calling me 'Buzz.' When can I jettison this cane? I'm afraid I'll trip over it."

Dr. Rosenblum peered at him over his glasses. "I suggest you use it when you take short walks with Sarge. The dog would enjoy that . . . and can always drag you home if you tumble. He is certainly getting big."

It seemed that Sarge now considered Dad's recovery his own special project. Mom said he rarely left Dad's side when I was at school.

The doctor leaned back in his chair as Mom brought in lemonade. "Now, I have a different proposal for Sarge, but this one includes Bobby." He glanced over at me. "Have you mentioned anything to your parents?"

"No, sir. It seemed too good to be true. I didn't want to count on it."

"Well, let's see what your parents think of my proposition." He turned to Mom and Dad. "Sarge is quite a remarkable dog, with the training your son has given him. Perhaps you noticed, Cap . . . , uh, Buzz, while you were at the hospital some of the work the therapists are doing using support dogs. There are so many patients who need help that they are quite overwhelmed. We could use Bobby and Sarge this summer to give them some relief. Would that be okay with you?"

Dad reached out to scratch Sarge's ears. "You want to take both of them to help at the hospital? How will that work? I mean getting them back and forth."

"My schedule fluctuates some, but it's nothing we can't work out. They can ride up with me and Ruth when I drive up. I can arrange for them to stay overnight, at times, or find transportation to get them home. The therapists are looking forward to meeting them. Bobby would be working directly with those folks. He would, of course, be paid quite well . . . and fed while he's there."

My parents looked at each other, and then at me and Sarge. I was glad I hadn't mentioned it to them. Mom spoke first. "Bobby, you already knew about this. Is this something you would like to do?"

"Yeah, I knew, but I wasn't sure it would really happen. I'd love to do it. Sarge is well trained, but I'm sure he can learn more. I did see some of those wounded soldiers. I'd like to help if I can."

"Well, this is a wonderful opportunity to help, Bobby," Dad said. "I guess your Mom and I can lend you out for the summer." He looked really proud.

Dr. Rosenblum picked up his black satchel and stood to leave. "That is good news. School will be out before long. Gives us time to coordinate a workable schedule for everyone. Those hospital people will be delighted with the news." He nodded at Mom. "You are doing a good job of keeping Buzz on task."

Dad stood to walk him to the door. "She threatens to send me back to have the nurses boss me around if I don't mind her." He had his arm around Mom. And it was the left one.

▲ ▲ ▲

I stood at the project table and tapped the weather coating I'd brushed on Mom's birdhouse to see if it was still tacky.

Mr. Swanson walked over. "I checked, too, Bobby. I think it's fine to add a couple hooks to hang it from a tree or porch. You did a great job."

"Thanks. My mom will love it."

"Oh, I almost forgot. I got a note from your friend Arnie. He sent it to the school." The teacher handed the envelope to me.

Arnie had always seemed like such an oaf, I was surprised he would even *think* about writing, let alone really do it. I read the note:

Hi, Bobby,

I like farm life, speshally granddad's animals. One of the dogs reely likes me. Her name is Gypsy and she sleeps in my room. I got started in school here and made a cupple friends. But your my best friend.

I talked to the band teacher and can get into the summer band program. He said I probly have enuf air to blow a tuba or trumpet. Told the football coach I was two busy with music to play sports but I will be in the pep band.

I hope you fixed the birdhouse. Also that your dad is getting okay. Pat Sarge for me. Rite if you can.

Your buddy,

Arnie

Mr. Swanson was watching me. "Is he doing okay, Bobby? I'm glad you boys worked things out. I did hear about his dad's problem. Guess he's still in jail."

I handed the note for him to read. He smiled when he handed it back. "Let's hope a good English teacher gets ahold of him, too."

CHAPTER 35

A Setback

Dad's first couple weeks home went well. Mom wore the cap of Master Sergeant well—or so Dad complained with a smile. "I tell you, Bobby, she's worse than any boot-camp sarge in the military. All I hear is: *Time for exercises*, or *take this pill*, or *nap time*."

Mom kissed the top of his head. "Bobby, think you can teach Sarge to nip Dad's heels when he balks at naps?"

Hearing the word *sarge* over and over, my dog sat at attention and saluted. We all laughed. "Dad, you don't know how often Don and I tried to get Sarge to salute us, and all he did was wag his tail. The first time he did it was when you came home, and everyone saluted you. Now, he does it all the time."

"I think he's in cahoots with your mom to keep me in line. Uh, oh—it must be time for my Saturday-afternoon nap. I see Mom motioning me into the bedroom."

After getting Dad settled into bed, Mom whispered to me. "I'm going to lie down with him. He drifts off to sleep better if he's not alone."

"That's okay, Mom. I have that new model plane I want to work on." I motioned to Sarge. "C'mon—you can help me."

About a half hour later, I was pinning some balsa strips into place when Sarge sprang off his rug and stood in the doorway, both ears cocked. Then he padded down the hallway to my parents' room. I was right behind him, hearing Dad's confused voice and Mom's soothing one. I tapped on the door and pushed it open.

Dad was sitting on the edge of the bed, frightened eyes flitting back and forth. "Where are we, Midge? Have they found us? I can't go back in there. I won't!" He looked terrified.

Mom sat next to him and rubbed his hands. "You're safe, Buzz. You're home now. Those times were long ago."

Sarge padded over and rested his head on Dad's knee, making soothing dog noises. I watched as Dad rubbed his ears, smiled, and said. "You are persistent for a dog, but, no, you cannot take a nap with me."

Mom appeared with a glass of water. "Time for a pill, Buzz."

Dad saluted her. "Yes sir. Is this for my shoulder, my head . . . or maybe my toe or little finger?"

Mom gave him a look. "Dr. Rosenblum says it's good for whatever is wrong with you. I may ask for some for myself. You lie back down for a bit longer."

She ushered me and Sarge out and closed the door. Exhaling a deep breath, she motioned me to step out onto the porch with her.

Relaxing into an old rocker set out for Dad to use, she looked up at me and smiled. "Yes, Bobby, we are having some episodes like this. Dr. Rosenblum told me they would come during his sleep from time to time. He called them *flashbacks* to his times as a POW and on the escape route with the Resistance. Being wounded as he was only intensified the experience." She reached her hand up to me as I hitched myself on the porch railing. "I'm to stay calm, reassuring him he is *safe* and *home*."

"Golly, Mom, I didn't know. Has he done this much?"

"Only a few times at night. I'm learning how to calm him until he snaps out of them. You and I need to remember that he had not lived in this house with us but a few months before he was shipped overseas. All he's known is constant, regulated military life, even at the hospital. He needs to get used to home life again so that he can let the other go."

"Will you two be okay if I'm away at the hospital this summer? I don't have to go if you need me."

"If I need you, I know where you are. This is a wonderful opportunity for you, Bobby. Dad is so proud of you. He wouldn't want to be the reason you miss it."

"You know, Mom, I remember times at the hospital when it was like he'd left us and was someplace else. He seemed so distant that it was scary."

Mom leaned back and rocked a bit. "Yes, I think that's still happening—but only when he's asleep. Dr. Rosenblum thinks that, as he gets used to home, those episodes will fade over time."

"I feel sad for Dr. Rosenblum and Ruth with the mom still in Austria with her parents. Do you think we could invite them over for supper some evening and just a visit? You know, not a check-up on Dad. More of a fun time."

"That's a great idea, Bobby. Let me check my ration stamps, and I'll invite our good doctor and Ruth at his next visit here."

CHAPTER 36

Just Being Social

Two weeks later

Sarge raced to the door. Ears pricked and tail wagging dangerously, he did remember to sit. Dad opened the door and welcomed Dr. Rosenblum and Ruth. Not to be outdone, Sarge lifted a paw to shake hands. Ruth dropped to the floor to take the paw and rub his ears. "Hello, there, my favorite dog," she said.

"Hi, Ruth," I said. "Glad you're here. Come see my latest airplane model." I hustled her down the hall. "I have to make sure I capped the glue properly, or I'll never get it open next time."

She paused in the bedroom doorway to take in all my planes hanging from the ceiling. "What does your new one look like?"

"It's a British Hurricane. I think I have about exhausted American models." I stood back so she could see. "Next time, I'll try one of the German planes. A Messerschmidt, I think."

"These are great, Bobby. My Papa needs to see." She returned with Dr. Rosenblum in tow.

"Very nice, Bobby. It seems that once you get involved in an activity, you stick with it. You must put Sarge through his paces while I am here."

Ruth had snatched my checker-game as she left my room. "I just know I can beat you today."

She led me out to our front porch, where we set the board up on an old table. A bird swooped past her head.

"You have to be careful out here, Ruth." I motioned to mom's new birdhouse hanging from a tree. "The bluebirds have set up housekeeping."

"Oh, that's the house you built at school?"

"Yeah. I gave it to Mom for Mother's Day. She was pretty happy. The birds are, too."

Ruth clenched her hands under her chin, eyes dancing. "Bobby, we got such marvelous news." A brief cloud darkened her face. "Or, *most* of it is marvelous."

"What's going on, Ruth?"

"I have good news and some not so good. My mother will leave Austria as soon as she can find a way, or people to help her. We do not know how, but I hope soon. The not-so-good is that my grandpapa died from pneumonia. When the Nazis beat him, some ribs were broken, and he did not recover. Medical care is limited, especially for the older people."

"That's terrible, Ruth. What about your grandmother?"

"My *Mutti* has three brothers. All were in the military. The oldest one was injured and is home. He has taken her in. She can help with their *Kinder*. That will make her happy—and to be useful." Ruth brightened. "Now, my *Mutti* can join us in America."

"Won't that be dangerous for her, trying to get out on her own?"

"Everything is dangerous over there, Bobby. But, as Papa says, there is no problem that can't be solved."

"Ruth, he told me those very same words. I hope your mother finds a way here soon, and safely." I grinned at her. "No wonder you seemed to be on wings today."

"Papa is working with the Jewish agencies, the Red Cross, and anyone else he can think of. We can hardly wait to see her again."

Ruth was so starry-eyed that I relaxed my strategies to let her win a few games of checkers. Then Mom called us in for supper.

Now that Dr. Rosenblum was calling Dad "Buzz," he insisted Dad refer to him as "Isaac." "It is good to visit people and not be the doctor for an evening," he said and turned to Ruth. "Did you tell Bobby our good news?"

"Oh, yes," Ruth said. "I can't wait to see Mutti again. I just hope it won't take too long for her to find a way."

"That's great news, Ruth," Mom said. "I look forward to meeting your mom. I just wish there was some way we could help." She carried plates to the sink.

"Hey, Honey," Dad said. "Do you have enough cobbler for the McDowells? Brian might have some ideas."

Mom gave him a sassy look. "I made two of them. How much do you plan to eat, Captain Bradley?"

He got up to go to the phone, shaking his head. "I'll restrain myself if I must."

My parents' bantering made me smile.

Within minutes, Sharon was knocking on the door, and the McDowell family entered. Mom already had her cobbler dished up and her treasured coffee perking on the stove. I loved hearing chatter around the table. It had been missing for so long.

Ever thoughtful, Ruth asked what games we had to include Sharon. We settled on *Battleship,* and the six-year-old quickly caught on. I could hear the adults fielding ideas that might help accelerate Mrs. Rosenblum's journey to this country. I knew Major McDowell had useful connections to cut through restrictions and red tape. "What's in her favor is that she is Austrian and not German. Also, that there is family here in the States to vouch and provide for her," Major McDowell said. "Let me check how best to proceed. I'll talk with some of my contacts who may know someone who knows someone else. We'll be glad to help, Dr. Rosenblum . . . uh, I mean Isaac."

Though summer was on its way, it was getting dark outside when the crowd get-together broke up. Little Sharon gathered up the cards to put back in the boxes. "Thanks for letting me play. I like playing with you big peoples. Donnie always lets me win, but you don't." She gave her brother a teasing look.

"Well, that's over, Sharon," Don said as he jerked a pigtail. "You'll have to hold your own from now on."

CHAPTER 37

SECRETS ARE OUT

A month later

Dr. Rosenblum dropped me at our front gate. I opened the car's back door to let Sarge out.

"Thanks for the ride. Today was great. See you Monday."

Sarge sat while I opened the gate, but his attention was on the hearty laughter emerging through the front screen door. I stood with him, listening. I knew I'd heard that laugh before, but when and where?

I entered the house to find Mom, Dad, and a uniformed stranger laughing over something. Dad motioned me over. "Do you happen to remember who this is, Bobby? It's been a while."

"The laugh. I remember that laugh, Dad. Is this Smitty?"

The man stood to shake hands, "Great to see you again, Bobby, but you've put a lot of altitude between your shoes and that butch haircut since our last meet. Captain J. P. Smit. To be precise, Captain Jeremiah Percival Smit." He released a big laugh. "Any wonder that I go by 'Smitty'?"

Dad rose. "Before I forget, Smitty, come take a look at Bobby's fleet of air power." He led his friend to my bedroom.

The British Hurricane now hung from the ceiling; a partially finished German Messerschmidt was on my worktable. The two men silently studied my planes. Were those tears in their eyes? Smitty turned to the table. "Oh, yes. A Messerschmidt Bf109. Good planes. I shot quite a few of those down."

"Aren't we glad *that's* behind us?" Dad guided his friend back to the kitchen. "How about another piece of pie?"

"Oh, no. Midge did a good job of filling me up. But, I would like to hear about Bobby's dog."

I explained how I happened to get Sarge. Then I put him through his paces and explained the work we would be doing at the hospital through the summer.

"So, you guess Sarge may have been destined for work with the MPs? He's certainly big enough to get anyone's attention," Smitty said.

Before I realized it, I'd told them about how he took down Arnie's dad, never backing down. "He was just amazing. He knew exactly what he had to do to stop the beating and went for it. I was so proud of him."

Mom and Dad looked dumbfounded. Smitty laughed. "Looks like this is news to your parents, Bobby. What happened to the guy?"

Mom's hand covered her mouth, but Dad was nodding. "You two seem to be quite the team, Bobby. Better tell us the end of the story."

"I think Mr. Larsen is still in jail or prison. It seemed he was afraid to tell who the other Black Marketeers were. The family moved to Idaho to live with grandparents."

"And, this son was the one who shot Sarge?" Dad asked.

So then I told Arnie's story and about getting a letter from him later.

"Good way for that to all work out, Bobby." Dad was nodding his head.

"I just wish we'd had Sarge last year," Mom said. She got flustered when she realized she'd finally let our story out of the bag.

Dad turned to look at her and then at me. "What happened last year while I was overseas, Midge?" Mom remained quiet. "Bobby, maybe you better be the storyteller."

"Well, Dad, you've met Laura Ann. It began with her . . ." It took an hour to tell about our boarder-assistant scout leader-substitute teacher, Laura Ann's suspicions, and the scary night in the alley.

"I'll be darned," Dad said over and over.

"I didn't write you, Buzz, because I wanted you to concentrate on keeping yourself safe," Mom explained. "We were safe enough here. It was just awkward. Bobby never left me alone."

Smitty slapped Dad on the back and released one of his big laughs. "And, you and I thought the war was in Europe. Seems lots was happening on the Home Front." He looked at Midge. "I think this calls for another piece of pie before I get back to base."

The man with the big laugh left with promises to keep in touch. And, Dad? He kept asking questions about the Black Market episode and again and again about the Nazi spy.

No one noticed Sarge snoring on the couch . . . again. Or maybe no one cared.

CHAPTER 38

ONE YEAR LATER
June 1945

Sarge and I were about to begin our second summer working in the physical-therapy section of the hospital. I'd enjoyed last summer. Sarge and I both learned a lot. Watching the wounded men leave with their therapy dogs, big smiles on their faces, made me so proud to have helped.

Today Mom laid the law down. It was time to clean my room with a capital "C."

I started with my bookcase. Papers stuck out of books, tablets, and corners. I pulled everything off the shelves, sorted, and re-shelved my books. Papers and notebooks were next. Some were trashed until I got to the tablet containing the letters I had written Dad while he was away. What should I do with them?

I leaned back against my bed, Sarge's chin on my leg, to reread them. With each page I relived those moments, not all of them especially good memories. Did my Dad need to read these? How might they make him feel? I decided to write one last letter, seal them all in an envelope and stash it in a bottom drawer. I might like to read them myself years from now.

June, 1945
Hello Future!

I'm just-turned-seventeen. My German shepherd dog, Sarge, is going on four. My Dad is doing what he does best again—training new pilots out at Hill Air Base.

Our family has experienced some scary times due to this war. As a pilot, Dad was sent to England to train new pilots and work with instrument flying. It gets so foggy over there. Mom and I did pretty well, just the two of us. Somehow, we wound up with a man living in an attic room, and he even ate with us. Housing shortage, we were told. Quite an adventure Laura Ann, Don, and I had exposing him as a Nazi spy. Have no idea what happened to him. Perhaps Germany will get him back.

Then, on an instrument-testing mission, Dad was shot down over France; spent time in a German POW camp; escaped, courtesy of the French Resistance; and recovered from serious shrapnel wounds at the hospital in Brigham City. Mom and I are so happy to have him home safe and well again. So happy, I guess, that I will be welcoming a baby brother or sister next month. I'm not fussy about which "flavor," but I suspect Mom would like a baby girl. She was raised with three older brothers.

Sarge was brave enough to face down Arnie's dad, who was involved with dealing gasoline on the Black Market. That was a scary evening. The dad was in prison last I heard, reluctant to reveal his accomplices. Arnie, his mom, and his sister were happy to move to Idaho to live with grandparents. We keep in touch from time to time.

Last summer and, now again this year, Sarge and I will be working with the therapists at the hospital, training veterans and their dogs to work together. It's a great job, and I even get paid. Becoming a physical therapist is something I am considering. Dr. Rosenblum, who led me into this work, has been quite a figure in this family's world.

First, he helped Sarge when he was shot by Arnie, who thought he was a coyote. Then Dr. Rosenblum did both surgeries on my Dad—his shoulder and his head. Mom and I were so worried during those operations. On top of that, he helped Dad through some scary nightmares over his capture, being a POW, and then escaping. Dr. Rosenblum and his daughter had to leave Austria when the Nazis moved in.

His daughter Ruth became a good friend of mine. As her mom had stayed behind in Austria to help the grandparents, it was quite an operation to finally get her stateside. This past year Ruth has been attending school with Laura Ann, Don, and me in Ogden. That family is glad to be together again.

Ruth and Laura Ann are having a good time speaking German with Laura Ann's grandfather now that he has rejoined that family. He did elect to live in the "mouse house" trailer unless the snow is too deep and it gets too cold.

Dad's wingman Smitty stopped to visit a couple more times when he was at the base. I love to hear that guy laugh. Makes me happy inside. He and Dad can tell story after story. It seems easier for Dad to share his exploits in the war with Smitty around.

My best friend, Don, will be moving away this summer. His dad will assume new duties back in Washington, DC. I will really miss him. I have been invited to visit them there after we graduate next year. What a special trip that will be!

And this war! It seemed to go on and on, upsetting so many lives. Hitler, the coward, killed himself after leaving his own country and much of Europe in ruins. Germany surrendered a couple weeks ago. Japan is still fighting, but there are hopes that will end soon, too. April was a tough month for world leaders. Though Hitler killed himself, Mussolini was executed. President Roosevelt saw us through this war but died also. Our new president is Harry Truman.

The world is looking forward to the end of this war. So many lives have been lost and disrupted. When I see in the newsreels the devastation in other parts of the world, I am thankful it didn't reach America. Living with shortages and rationing seems a small price to pay. Perhaps when I read all these letters in future years, peace will have come to stay.

Signing off for now, Bob Bradley

BUSHNELL MILITARY HOSPITAL

Bushnell Military Hospital. Brigham City, Utah.
(Photo can be found on Utah State University digital exhibits.)
Image-lib.utah.edu/ark:/87278/s64jllpl

Author's note: This hospital was specifically built for the wounded GIs returning from the battlefield. It specialized in treating amputees, facial surgery, and neuropsychological conditions, and was the first military hospital to make use of penicillin.

For my story's purpose, it was well situated to help Bobby's dad. I took liberties regarding transportation for families who could not live close-by. The van is my invention to get Bobby and his Mom to visit Buzz. Dr. Rosenblum and his side story were a help to both Sarge and Buzz.

I could find no record pertaining to a physical-therapy program, so I invented one for the book. It made sense that the hospital would have those services available to amputees and other injured.

ABOUT THE AUTHOR

Mary. L. Routh-Brodie, retired schoolteacher, traded her red pencil for a computer, and her pupils for you readers. For ten years, she wrote a popular newspaper column while working on her novels. The setting and some events are lifted from childhood experiences during WWII, but Laura Ann, Bobby, Don, Ruth and Arnie fill the pages with their own stories.

When not writing, Mary quilts for her grandkids, refills a seed kitchen for her feathered friends, terrorizes the local trout population, and hangs out at the county library. Her adopted Papillion, Bonnie, keeps her on task with her story-telling from their family log cabin in Wyoming's Wind River Mountains.

Email her at marybrodie776@yahoo.com with questions or comments. She would love to hear from you.

I HOPE YOU ENJOYED THIS BOOK.

Would you do me a favor?

Like all authors, I rely on online reviews to encourage future sales. Your opinion is invaluable. Would you take a few moments now to share your assessment of my book at the review site of your choice? Your opinion will help the book marketplace become more transparent and useful to all.

Thank you very much!

9 781735 553023